Dear Digby

CAROL MUSKE-DUKES

Viking

VIKING
Published by the Penguin Group
Viking Penguin Inc., 40 West 23rd Street,
New York, New York 10010, U.S.A.
Penguin Books Ltd, 27 Wrights Lane,
London W8 5TZ, England
Penguin Books, Australia Ltd, Ringwood,
Victoria, Australia
Penguin Books Canada Ltd, 2801 John Street,
Markham, Ontario, Canada L3R 1B4
Penguin Books (N.Z.) Ltd, 182–190 Wairau Road,
Auckland 10, New Zealand

Penguin Books, Registered Offices:
Harmondsworth, Middlesex, England

First published in 1989 by Viking Penguin Inc.
Published simultaneously in Canada

1 3 5 7 9 10 8 6 4 2

Grateful acknowledgment is made for permission to reprint an excerpt
from "A Boy Like That" by Leonard Bernstein and Stephen Sondheim.
© 1957 Leonard Bernstein and Stephen Sondheim (renewed). All rights
controlled by Chappell & Co. and Amberson Enterprises. All rights
reserved. Used by permission.

LIBRARY OF CONGRESS CATALOGING-IN-PUBLICATION DATA
Muske-Dukes, Carol, 1945–
Dear Digby.
I. Title.
PS3563.U837D43   1989   813'.54   88-40285
ISBN 0-670-82506-9

Printed in the United States of America
Set in Linotron Palatino
Designed by Kathryn Parise

*For Laurie Frank and
my daughter, Annie Cameron*

*"The pure products of America
go crazy—"*
WILLIAM CARLOS WILLIAMS

I wish to thank the following individuals for their generous assistance and editorial and/or moral support: Lois Sortedahl, Dawn Seferian, Nan Graham, Laurie Frank, John Irving, Leo Braudy, Dorothy Braudy, Lynne McMahon, Cathy Bos, Andrew Fishmann, M.D., M. E. Loree Fishmann, Lee Shallat, Michael Ryan, Mimi Kennedy, Stuart Dawrs, Wendi Robbins, Martha Millard.

I especially want to thank David Dukes, for love, support, patience—and for driving me to Todi.

One

At the top of the Wandstar Building, high above Manhattan, dwarfing the towers of Chrysler and Pan Am, are the offices of SISTERHOOD magazine, commonly known as SIS. In the late rays of cocktail hour, the SIS windows purple like stained glass, and till dawn the rotating red SIS logo (the bio-sign of the female, with an S curled inside) glows reassuringly as a lighthouse beacon, a neon night-light. For others, though, it's a migraine, unsettling sleep as it circles: a bloodthirsty bat on a rafter.

I ought to know. For five years I've been letters editor at SIS. Every day I ride the elevator to 72, press the security buzzer, nod to the bronze SIS logo and Minnie White-White-Goldfarb, the hyphenated receptionist, pass the Situation Room and Day Care—on my way to my little red desk, piled high with scrawled letters to the editor.

SIS is a new kind of magazine for women. A magazine for that generation of changelings called the Independent Woman. Our covers usher in the New Woman in a series of role models, mother goddesses, psychological bricklayers.

The Soviet woman cosmonaut. The IRA firebrand and Parliament member. The French head of Female Cultural Affairs. The Indian premier. The Greek Resistance fighter. We are an unheard-of representative medium: a national glossy with "matte" concerns, a bimonthly cross between a feminist *Time* and a liberated *Ladies Home Journal* with an all-woman staff serving a readership of five million. SIS is hot stuff. It comes close to having what men call power, but we at SIS never use that word.

I myself never use the word because I have no power. What I feel like is a clerk in some lost warehouse of the imagination. I sit for days sifting through sky-high stacks of postmarked dreams. There are letters on lime-green stationery with little yellow bunnies running down the margin, and letters on paper with photos of smiling ape heads in the upper left-hand corners reading: "Notes from a Profound Thinker," and letters pocked with teardrops, blood spots, bacon grease, semen. Every hour or so I put my head down on my desk and bump it casually. "My name is Willis Jane Digby," I say to myself, "Willis Jane Digby. And I am a sane person." But I'm not convinced.

It is my opinion that I am going mad in the capacity of letters editor. The letters themselves started out being amusing, then disturbing, then haunting, then capable of driving me slowly (if that's possible at the rate of ten thousand per month) out of my mind. I felt that I had come to recognize in their diabolical styles, in their terrible false heartiness and conspiratorial tone, the unmistakable echo of our own SIS style; in certain of them I've come to recognize the mirror image shot back in our eyes by shards of glass, clear breakage. I sit with my head in my hands and feel the successive flashes like gunfire.

Certainly the sanity of the average reader of SIS has often been called into question by establishment shrinks. We publish articles on Getting to Know Your Cervix, complete with a couple of sisters sitting around with hand mirrors earnestly comparing labial puckers and yawns; we solemnly discuss nonsexist parts of speech, including "na" and "nu," the liberated pronouns; our list of suggested Christmas gifts for the Free Woman includes a bronzed diaphragm, a trophy. Was it such a big step to the woman who wrote in that she was sexually harassed by the bald man on her can of oven cleaner? Or the one who complained to us that a tiny orthodox rabbi entered and vacated her vagina at will?

Well, okay, maybe a *big* step for *man*kind, but for womankind it seemed smaller, a lateral move, a sidestep. I've known so-called crazy women all my life (haven't you?): the ravers in supermarkets, the savers of string and old nylon stockings (whose hoard soon filled rooms!), the nonstop talkers, the depression shoppers, the neighborhood kook with rouge spots and old Christmas bows in her hair, bag ladies, bugged slaves of the spotless house, polishers of the same spot on the piano. *My mother*, one hot June day in 1959, throwing the iron out the window, and yelling after, "Ironing drives me *nuts*, did you hear that, Mrs. Comstock???"

Male crazies come in predictable (often boring) wrappers, but the women are chattier, more distracted from the solemnity of dementia—hearing six voices at once (like a mother!) and still talking, jugglers of thought–hors d'oeuvres, hearers of stereo prayers, weirdly *hopeful* in a hopeless world. Coupon snippers, shoplifters, crash dieters, home decorators, jingle thinker-uppers, the occasional baby smotherer who did it for love.

Well, I (with reservations) salute them. The stuff from men really gets on my nerves sometimes. I read letters from deranged, vindictive males aloud at editorial meetings amid great protest; I post them in the john. But the women's stuff I take home with me, sometimes; I read their letters over a cup of hot tea, nodding, shaking my head, feeling for us all.

So here I sit, lonely hearts joker, at my little red desk. Where my job is to read (with a few fast-disappearing assistants) *every letter*. To answer each with at least a form reply. To select a few of the more sane for publication in the Letters column. To get back to those that seem to warrant either an official or semipersonal response.

On an average day I find my IN box bristling with envelopes. First come the run-of-the-mill cheerleaders—"keep up the good work, sisters"—and general commentary from both sexes: intelligent, thoughtful letters about child care centers, prenuptial contracts. Then comes the first level of Ink Theater:

Hey Female Libbers of the World—Thought for the Day on the Subject of Rape (or what *I* call Got Lucky Sex!): GET POKED, DOLORES! Do you hear guys going around pretending to know anything about being Knocked Up and feeling like a Blind Dumb Sow? Do I give you advice on Cramps? Then why is it you chicks act like you know what it's like to get a nice steaming whopper of Semen delivered free to your testiculs with No Where to Unload???

If enough loads pile up, Sister, a Guy can get Pissed. Real Pissed.

Upshot: Walk a mile in my Jockstrap, Yolanda.

I'd like to drop by SIS and show you all this process, how it works, but I got my third leg in traction right now. It gets thrown out of joint because of its size. But I got a few Hot Loads comin' up. You'll know me when you see me, girls.

XXXXX
Dino Pedrelli

Dear Reader,

SIS thanks you for your letter. Unfortunately, due to the volume of our correspondence, it is impossible to answer each letter personally. However, we will place your letter in our files and look forward to your continued interest in SIS.

In struggle,
Willis J. Digby, Letters Ed.

P.S. Dino:

Impotency is a common enough male sexual dysfunction. Don't let it getcha down. Traction sounds like the most intimate relationship you'll ever get. Hang in there, pal.

WJD

You see, I've actually begun to *answer* the weirdest letters. I think about them all the time, but the transition from thought to paper is a major shift. I have a pair of Bugs Bunny rabbit ears attached to a wire halo that I put on when I feel in the mood to respond to the Loonies. On the days when I also wear my three-piece pinstripe suits and ties, or my tux, I feel immortal—the way the authors of those letters feel righteous, deathless, sublimely inspired. I like looking weird; I've found that it gives me confidence. People look, laugh uncertainly, then watch their step with me. I look up from a stack of letters, the rabbit ears wobbling, and I loosen my tie just a little and frown. That gets them.

Because of my first name (for the Willis my father expected as first son in my place), I get a lot of letters from guys who think I'm odd man out at SIS. Good Old Willy Digby.

Dear Willis,

Don't know what you're doing there, comrade, but I thought I'd write to you, who must suffer much at the hands of those Amazons.

I am a youthful, personable, impeccable-looking dentist (twenty-eight and a full-fledged D.D.S.), and I ride my bicycle to my office each day to keep fit. One morning I'd paused at a STOP sign (I, of course, obey all posted traffic regulations!) when a young woman (we shall *not* refer to her as a "girl") about twenty-three or so passed in front of me. Her bow-shaped lips were smiling in a little smile, which I took to be an acknowledgment of me. (Though maybe she was smiling to herself?) At any rate, as she sashayed in front of me, swinging her hips in girlish fashion, I called out in a jovial tone (and without, I believe, a trace of sexual innuendo), "Hello, my lovely!" and I flashed her what I think was an energetic but neutral grin.

Now prepare yourself. She stared hard back at me and said in a calm, even polite voice, "Why don't you take this and light up your asshole, you smarmy little twerp!" Then she threw her lit cigarette at my bicycle seat and marched off.

Well. I went to my office and gave myself a good blast of nitrous oxide. (Laughing gas, to you.) I'm still reeling as I write this, but I'm abjectly depressed. Daylight is about one-twentieth the size of New York, and if this sordidness can go on in Ohio, I shudder to think what you guys are going through there.

Willis, I think (if you can beat those harpies off the typesetting machine!) you should print this letter. I'm well aware of the official SIS line of propaganda regarding unsolicited male comments—but I'd like females everywhere to know how provocative their appearance

Carol Muske-Dukes

6

is to men, and to dentists. And how we're kicked in the teeth like this and still expected to come back for more! I am gassed, yes, *gassed* right now, and ready to drill any female I see (excepting my dental hygienist, who is above reproach), but I would be very grateful if my story came to light. Fight *vagina dentata*!

From: Badly-Gassed in Ohio

Dear Badly Gassed,

I am not a man, but of the female persuasion myself. I do somewhat understand your position here, though. Prone. You sure must feel stupid. "Energetic but neutral"—Christ. I think you oughtta lay low for a while, stay gassed, and sell that bike. The image of a sexually aroused dentist is never a happy one.

Yrs,

WJD, Tooth Fairy

Listen Up, CUNTS!

Your Rich-Bitch politics suck a big weenie!

SIS is in bed with all the corporate powers of the Pig Capitalist Structure! SIS gives head on Wall Street! You run silly ads telling women to paint their faces and fingernails and wear panty hose. You support the use of feminine hygiene products—with impunity! You shake one fist in the air in the Liberation salute while the other gives Max Factor a hand job!

Are you proud of this, SIS? Ask yourself: Would Che's sister have read SIS? Would Lenin's mother have subscribed? Mother Jones would have used SIS for t.p., you bovine big-bottomed bourgeois bitches!

Who will liberate your neo-pussy rhetoric, SIS? Let's

get REAL, SIS, let's hang those flabby tits and armchair asses out the Window of Life—and shoot the breeze with the masses!

Those who are out to destroy your hypocrisy will roll over on you in the end! I suggest that you wake up now, before it's too late, and invest some of your ripped-off profits where they can effect real Social Change. Send your bank-authorized check immediately to me care of my Institute.

THE RANDOLPH JORGE TUTMYER FOUNDATION
Randolph Jorge Tutmyer, Exec. Director
P.O. Box 69
Yorba Linda, CA.

Dear Randy (or may I call you Tut, Tut?),

Sorry, no handouts. We need all our money for breast augmentation. Big overhead, you might say.

WJB
Armchair Editor

Dear Mere Women,

Ever since Adam and Eve (that ballbreaker!), women have been trying to prove that they are superior to men. Men, of course, have never had to prove their superiority (it's writ On High!). While chuckling over this unarguable Fact of Nature just the other day, I realized that we men have had, all this time, indisputable proof! And here it is: FLASHING is an occupation wherein men play Hard Ball and leave women choking on their exhausts!!! You wimpy little women libbers can't reply when the world asks: Where are all the female flashers? Everyone knows that men are bolder, more death-defying by nature. Women are shy, cringing little pipsqueaks who should never attempt to become telephone repairmen or men's room attendants. These are jobs that require guts and savvy and women just don't have these things—no matter how much they blab about equality! Women say they are being kept back. Well, my dears, males are leaving you behind in the bulrushes in the field of flashing, and nobody is keeping you back from doing it. I'm *proud* most flashers are men. Still, I wouldn't mind seeing a woman rapidly ascend through the ranks of flashers.

Don't get me wrong: I'm not saying that if a woman gets out and flashes she will become head of a large conglomerate or President of the U.S., or something. Flashing expresses the individual in one's being, and women's bodies (let's face it) are just not that individual. Their bodies are woefully inferior to men's, they sag in many places, and the most disgusting thing is, they shake like a bowlful of Jell-O when they run across a room naked! Have you ever noticed? This is why the public stands one hundred percent behind its male flashers! If you met a real flasher in a side street, you'd probably scream at his statuesque form, his lithe churning hips—and his proud hello! You'd run shrieking off for the police, you fat, fully clothed inferior chicks!

Sincerely,
Desmond Blatz

I did hear from a number of fat, fully clothed inferior chicks. Those on the track of sexist symbology wrote in regularly with new findings:

Dear Editors,

I've had it! Take a gander at the logo below.

NORTH AMERICAN TRACKLINES

Do you see what I see? Well, if you don't, you're blind as a bat! Any hapless, train-riding wanker can see this subconscious sex symbol for what it is, to wit: a huge, hot, fully erect penile gland being rammed into a calm but retracting vagina! Thank you, Perversion Central (our friendly Advertising Industry), for this big gratuitous bone tossed smack into the slavering jaws of America's rapists!

Please! Peruse this gonad gestalt! Realize, please, that now any ad-reading commuter–pervert who wants to cream his pants on the way home—can!! It's a short track from this eye-popper to Rape itself. Meanwhile, he's riding high, and he's headed your way—this loose cannon, this venereal Crab on a fast-rolling P-word-on-Wheels!

I think I've said all that I need to say here, but I would appreciate your further investigation of the origins of this depraved violent visual assault. Remember, I wish to be kept posted!

Yours,
Mona de Rowster

Dear Mona,

Thanks a lot for alerting us here at SIS to this sexist marketing technique. However, I think that the penis-on-wheels notion is going just a bit far. I have to catch the 5:10 pecker to Scarsdale today, and knowing Namtrak, all we can count on them for is premature ejaculation.

Yours in struggle,
Willis Digby

I imagine you're getting the idea now. Still, one letter I set aside as a kind of Weirdometer—I started rating the letters 1 to 5, 5 being the weirdest, based on the following letter as a 6. The letter was from Iris Moss.

Iris Moss was a little cagey about her residence, but it became apparent that she lived a brave life significantly restricted by the state or other concerned parties. While, in the main, Iris's concerns were not mine, I felt a reverence for her obsessions, which began to feed into my own. Her style of thought grew on me.

Iris L. Moss
44 Gardenia St.
The Clark Building
Easterby, N.Y.
11:17 A.M.

Dear SIS magazine,

Over the years you've published a lot of articles I've liked. Recently you published one entitled "Why I Stay Single"—I *think* that was the name of it! I was very impressed by the author's viewpoints on the subject of why she never married and why she never wished to marry. I would like very much to share with you my own reasons for remaining single and for insisting on my own spouse-free space.

Mine, as everyone will admit, is a fascinating story, and I would be delighted to accept monetary renumeration for it. If, on the other hand, you don't want to print my story—I'll give it to you as a gift. By all means, retain it for purposes of educating other women to be as liberated as I am.

What is marriage? I have no idea!!! I also had no idea previously—because no one actually asked me to be his wife. Then, eventually, one or two did (against my will!).

One of these suitors happened to be Donald Irifune, ex-bonsai salesman and an executive-in-training at Baskin-Robbins, who asked me to marry him once while serving me a Big Mocha with jujubes—but he lost a finger in the Osterizer roughly five seconds after speaking—so I assumed that the offer would not stand up in court.

Then an old, very old man proposed to me in New York City: Ollie Mutzner. Ollie Mutzner was in a Special Geriatric Wing—sometimes in a wheelchair and occasionally on a respirator—but don't let this fool you—he was a pistol!! Mr. Mutzner was a glittering bon vivant, a TV personality with his own cable access channel! What an M.C.!

He personally trained and introduced many of the Socko Senior Tumblers, including the world-famous Mrs. Fanny Wallatuse, but that is another story. Mr. Mutzner proposed to me on fifteen different occasions, but being a foolish young thing, I was put off by certain of his physical characteristics, you know, like long nose hairs and the self-conscious manner in which he sang "Feelings."

Often I've regretted this youthful decision, but since Ollie Mutzner went into a coma not long after the last proposal (though I've heard he *still* does his show!), I think our life together might have been too explosive. We're both Leos, which has to be faced.

Not long after my brief fling with Ollie Mutzner, I

met a lad who laid carpet for Christ—or so he said. His name was Ronnie Larsk and he was Born Again. I was not. I usually find that being born once is entirely sufficient for a person. So we did not get along well from the first, ideologically speaking, yet I was attracted to his evangelical fire (which sometimes I admit was plain indigestion—the man had terrific Gas) and though I've always been an agnostic with cosmopolitan tendencies myself, I respected his Fundamentalist chutzpah. He told me, quite movingly, about prayer meetings he attended where people demonstrated their piety by leaping in the air and calling and signaling for Jesus as if he were some divine headwaiter. He also spent time elaborating on the horrible fates of the Non-Saved, who would be crisped in hellfire like Pork Rinds. He also proposed, though in his eyes, I was in the Dark.

Ronnie and I broke off one day when he was laying Astro Turf at my place of residence and began speaking in tongues. He caused tremendous upset among the other residents (who began answering him in tongues) and caused further dismay by farting a great deal during this episode—since, as I mentioned, he was a victim of Gas and he had just consumed a typical lunch in our cafeteria (*Cuchifritos* and creamed corn). By the time the staff got the corridors cleared, he had locked himself in my room (with me), still farting and speaking in tongues. I found myself looking at Ron the way one does when the flame has died. It was becoming harder and harder to fit him into my life. So I struck him a few light karate blows* (about the face and chin, avoiding the gaseous abdomen), knocked him out, and opened the windows wide. It took hours to get Ronnie hauled away (in the meantime, I simply stowed him in a Hefty

---

* I'm a trained Black Belt.

bag), but the staff wanted to resuscitate him first. I won't go into it, but it took weeks (as you might imagine) to crank open the airlocks and bring my room back to normal.

Well. Those are my reasons for never marrying before this. Now here we have a dilemma—we're up to the present. Here I am, a woman of almost uncontainable sex appeal (and am I cognizant of it, you bet!) and a quicksilver mind and manner. I know the guy who got me would leap tall buildings at a single bound in gratitude. My face is haunting, and I have a pantherlike, smoothly coordinated body. I am brilliant and my conversation is original and scintillating. I know what it would mean to some poor Joe to hook me—PARADISIO! Yet I try to remain objective about it.

But there's something more to be considered. Let me put it this way. I know what is repugnant to me in another person, and I am committed to never being repugnant to another. Let me correct that: another blameless person. Naturally, if some bozo, out of nowhere, began forcing his penis into my vagina (under some weird trance or hypnosis), I would try very hard to be repugnant to him.

I would feel completely righteous if I suddenly came to (from the hypnosis) while he was shooting his sperm into my vagina—to eliminate him.

What right do these types have to go around hypnotizing women and blasting their seminal fluid up them? I've had my fill of this sort of thing in my life, and to deliver death to just one of these violators of my precious body would be the apex, the shimmering peak of my life. Think about it, would it not be of yours?

These attackers come out of the mist—sometimes in satanic garb and sometimes in doctor's uniforms—the average unsuspecting female has to be eternally vigilant.

You see, my underwear is my witness. I've been taking the time to sniff my panties a lot lately and, lo and behold!, I noticed that they reek of seminal fluid! What does this mean? It means, I suspect, that someone has been coming into my room to hypnotize me and pump huge quantities of sperm into my vagina. Then the perpetrator leaves me, spread-eagled there on the carpet, with seminal fluid pouring out from between my legs.

I've never seen these predator-fiends, but that's the way they work—you're hypnotized, *conk-ola*—then they hook up their pumpers.

I know what you're thinking: This woman does *not* like men. *Wrong.* I simply do not like the male member in my kit bag if I don't want it there. Got it? Simple enough to understand. The point is—I just don't want wet sperm trickling down my thighs every five minutes. I don't want to walk around all the time with a womb full of seminal fluid—or various strange penises—if I don't have to. It's a free country. If the lady is out for the count, don't stick it up. Simple enough to understand.

I love my room. It's quite beautiful, on the sunny side of the building with yucca and spider plants in the window. I am happy and peaceful in it. But, after the other night, when I awoke and felt seminal fluid gushing out of me, I put a big sign on my door:

WARNING LOCAL PENISES:
ARMED VAGINA BEYOND THIS POINT

Hypnotic rape is no fun. I added a P.S. to my sign stating that Basil Schrantz was the only man who would now be allowed to enter my room. I like Basil. I am fairly sure that he has no seminal fluid at all. Naturally, I do not wish to marry him. However, he is a helpful fellow who understands my strong sexual convictions and never asks about them. He comes in to talk and help me redecorate occasionally. I have my bed in different places: sometimes in the middle of the room, sometimes against the wall. The windows let in sun and cooling air, and I have the radio playing my favorites, which include Don Ho and Mabel Mercer. I put up a mirror or two occasionally, but not too many, because my beauty is distracting. I have a bulletin board with Peanuts cartoons and some of my favorite sayings from Socrates to R. D. Laing, and in the corner sits my desk and typewriter, where I write my letters. What else do I need? NOT SEMINAL FLUID!

I wasn't born yesterday! (Only the Born Again can say that!) I was born thirty-five years ago, and I know a gnocchi from an orange hat! Wait a minute—God's talking to me. She says that I would be thumb-sucking, drooling insane to ever want to change my life by matrimony. So now you have it: I enjoy the occasional companionship of Basil Schrantz. Once in a while, I even shake up a mean martini, which I share with God, and most important, I stand up valiantly and alone against the threat of seminal fluid. Got it? That's me in a nutshell!

So marry? That would be dumb, wouldn't it? The day I waltz down the aisle with some sperm-shooting yahoo, they can declare me a loony, put me in a hula skirt, and give me a free ride to the popcorn factory. I'm too far ahead of them all. I think of myself as a SIS cover: standing here in my room in full karate garb, the sun shining behind me, standing next to the warning on my door against the violators of my precious body—my

beautiful eyes, hair, teeth, breasts, yes! yes!—IRIS
MOSS, primo representative of the primo single state!
Hoping to hear from you soon,
Iris Moss

I could see Iris on the cover of SIS myself, sitting in her
lovely room with a pair of underpants over her head, waving
the paneled radio on the shelf broadcasting from Pluto,
plants percolating in their pots, the president's goonish
photo smirking out from the bulletin board tacked with
Snoopy figures, withered balloons, a rain of construction
paper exclamation points, yellowing articles clipped from
SIS. *Seminal fluid.*

Dear Iris,
SIS can't help you. SIS has the utmost sympathy for
most bodily secretions, but alas, little tradition of dealing
with seminal fluid. I too know, as an individual, what
it's like to feel happy, fairly content with one's life,
independent, etc.—and still feel like one is getting secretly fucked over. That's why I can't really help you
but can suggest only vigilance. Smoke a cigar after, smile
enigmatically, *stay awake.* You can fight this, Iris.

A large blue-and-green Nike, with a foot in it, appeared
on my desk. The shoe and foot belonged to Minnie White-
White-Goldfarb.
"Editorial meeting, Willis."
I looked up at her, hunched worriedly over her raised bent
knee, which was dimpled like a backside. She wrapped her
arms around the knee, a large anxious Germanic woman
with a big long nose and two huge yellow braids like a
Wagnerian heroine.
I felt great pity for Minnie White-White-Goldfarb because

she had more names than anyone I'd ever known. In her heart, Minnie'd felt obligated to hyphenate herself and her spouse, each surname like a chapter of a mystery novel. She's married a man named White—her own name had been White too. She could not bear the thought of "disappearing" into her husband's Whiteness. "It's like Eleanor Roosevelt," she was fond of saying. "How did she know *which* Roosevelt she was? When people asked for Eleanor Roosevelt, how could she determine if they wanted the Eleanor Roosevelt she was *before* marrying FDR (and maybe secretly still was!) or the Eleanor Roosevelt she was *after*? How could anyone tell if she really changed her name?" It *was* a hard question to answer. Minnie had finally solved her dilemma by keeping both names, her own and her husband's. She was Minnie White-White for a long while. Then her first husband was electrocuted in the bathtub when the answering machine fell into the bath water. "He'd put it right on the ledge above the tub," Minnie recalled sadly. "So he could monitor calls and pick up if he wanted. It was *terrible*—when I came in, the machine was half-floating, half-submerged, and the re-corded message kept repeating: "Greetings! This is Minnie White-White" ("*and* her hubby, Endor L. White!") "Guess what? We're not available to answer your call right now. . . ." She said the beep sound, like a drowning dol-phin's shriek, still haunted her dreams. After an appropriate period of mourning, Minnie married Amiri Goldfarb, the Arab-Jewish owner of the electronics parts store where she took the fatal answering machine to be fixed. They divorced a year later, but I'd heard rumors that a new name was about to be attached like an invisible Leggo to the series, the little arms of Goldfarb reached out for closure.

"This is an extremely happy time for me, Willis," she said. She looked alert but sad, as if a bad boy had put ice down her back. She began to cry.

I handed her a tissue. "Why?" I asked. I put Iris aside.

She cleared her throat. "I'm getting married. I'm marrying a wonderful guy. Salt of the earth. Get this: a Unitarian minister who plays mah-jongg *and* loves salsa!" She fumbled with a wad of Kleenex and blew her nose with a great beep.

She gave me a baleful look. "Gerard Biskell Rutgers-Oblonski." She waited for a reaction.

"Jesus," I said.

She cried softly for a while, then added: "Names are so easy for other people. They give up their history so readily, just sign a marriage license and all those years as somebody else are gone. I can't do that." She looked at me as if I headed the name-erasing conspiracy. "My fiancé's mother is English, his father is Polish. They wanted to preserve both strains."

She put the tissue back in her pocket. The six phone lines at the front desk, where she was supposed to be sitting, were lit up and squawking.

"God, I'm sick of names," she bellowed suddenly, and pulled her rubber sole, screeching, from my desk top. "I think I'm just going to call myself Number 208 or something."

"Why don't you just use your own name?"

"My *own* name? No woman owns her name! Anyway, *my* name was and is White, the same as my first husband. What good does that do me? I don't want to go back to that name, but I don't want a three-page driver's license either."

I pointed to the stack of letters on my desk, Iris's included.

"Here are some people with real problems."

Minnie shrugged and turned back to her phones.

"Yeah—but they're all crazy."

I sighed. The door to the Situation Room was opening and closing, editors wandered in, carrying notepads and flowered plastic coffee cups. I hurried in, late. Holly Partz, our editor in chief, had already begun to talk. I stumbled into a chair; I coughed loudly. Holly looked at me with exaggerated patience. I looked back at her. She was beautiful and brilliant, and she had invented SIS, then shared it with everyone. I hated her.

"Yes, Willis," she said. "What is it?"

"I think I'm going crazy."

There were boos and groans. Someone threw a crumpled napkin at me.

"C'mon, Willis, let's not start *this* again!"

"I'm going out of my mind," I said. "I cannot go on reading this stuff"—I waved some letters—"every day and stay sane."

"Willis. Take off your rabbit ears and the tux," said Marge Taggart. "You'll stay sane."

I looked at Marge. She was six feet tall and handsome. She smiled at me and winked.

"Marge, I think this job is for you. You've got the temperament."

"Willis." It was Holly—she was tapping her ballpoint against her big, square-faced watch. "Every issue your Letters section gets better. The letters you print are perfect, and your responses are funny and informative. What do you—"

"It's the ones we *don't* print I'm talking about. There are so many, I think we ought to publish some of them. I have a letter from a woman in Skyhigh, Utah, who thinks she's a Female Savior of the world. I'd just as soon pray to her as the Pope, wouldn't you? I'd like to say that in print."

Holly sighed. "Willis, what is your point? You know we can't print those letters."

"Why not?"

"You know why. The people who write those letters aren't well. Why would we make fun of them, humiliate them in a national magazine?"

"*They* wouldn't be humiliated. We would, right? We can't really admit that there are this many crazies out there who are responding passionately to our magazine. Isn't that it? And why can't our magazine also be for the woman who's gone a little crackers, alone in the rec room at ten A.M., eating Ding Dongs, getting weird?"

Page Kenney, my best friend, that traitor, gave me a bored look. "Willis, please sit down and shut up. Nobody cares about this but you."

"I know that, Page, thank you. That's what concerns me here. Why is it none of you are interested in a woman who is convinced that while she sleeps, strange men enter her and pump her full of *seminal fluid?*"

"Seminal fluid," said Marge Taggart. "Yuck."

"This woman wrote to SIS in response to *your* article, Marge, 'Why I Never Married'—she agreed wholeheartedly with you; she feels you think alike."

"Well, that figures, doesn't it? The whole *point* of my article was seminal fluid."

"I think Willis has a point." Everyone turned and looked over at Lupé Reyes. Lupé kept to herself a lot; there was a story around that she had been a child prostitute pimped by her own father. She came to the editorial meetings and sat silent most of the time. There was another rumor that she belonged to W.I.T.C.H., which stood for Women's International Terrorist Conspiracy from Hell. It was, as far as I knew, a kind of street theater group. I heard they did things like spray-paint SEXIST PIG on girlie posters and send dog poop quiches to Bobby Riggs.

"These so-called crazy women have a right to be heard." She got up and walked over to Marge and leaned against her chair. "A lot of people think Puerto Rican women are crazy—did you know that, Marge?"

"No," said Marge. "I didn't know that." She glared at me.

Lupé turned and looked at me too, a long, dark look.

"We can trust Willis to come up with something we all need to read about—isn't that right, Willis?"

I looked back at her, suddenly unsure. She smiled at me, very slow, very deliberate.

"I'd like to get back to our agenda here." Holly was standing on one foot, tapping her watch.

"I'd like to come up with a couple letters for the column," I said, "nothing shocking, just a glimpse of alternative approaches to reality."

Holly frowned and shook her head. "You worry me, Willis. But go ahead."

Then she turned back to her agenda, which included nominations for the next cover: so far we had Margaret Thatcher and Tina Turner. I waved at Page and slipped out for a drink of water.

Betty Berry was sitting at my desk. She was dressed, as usual, more oddly than me, and that was saying something. She looked like a collision in a boutique between Germaine Greer and General Westmoreland—she wore a kind of diaphanous dashiki with hiking boots. I never commented on her dress (since I was in no position to), and I'd always assumed her own style reflected some really satisfying personal fantasy. Like mine.

When I got closer, I saw that she was drinking Stolichnaya right out of the bottle and placed it, chilled and dribbling, right on Iris Moss.

She lifted the bottle as I approached, and I pulled Iris away—there were wet half-moons all over the page.

"I'm sorry, Willis," she croaked. "I'm sorry for taking over your desk and spilling on your papers. I'll get out of here."

She made no move, however, and I was forced to sit down in the chair across from my desk. I sponged Iris lightly with an envelope. Betty took another drink.

"Willis, remember when I called myself Betty Myrtlechild?"

Not names *again*, I thought. I couldn't take any more discussion of names.

"I just went through this with Minnie. . . ."

Betty made a face. "Minnie? Minnie's trying to annex a personal history; I was trying to escape my history. And give myself another identity."

"Your mom's name is Myrtle, right?"

"Right."

"Betty, don't get me wrong. But I know everything you're going to say here. You took your mother's name because you wanted to be free of the male patronymic and added 'child' to designate yourself, then I assume that you went back to your original name because you found Myrtlechild kind of a dumb name."

"You're partly right. The first part. I went back to Betty Berry because my children were embarrassed by the other name."

I looked at her. Children? I'd never known about any children—Betty was a lesbian. She looked like Gertrude Stein's sex therapist. Children?? I saw now how stupid I'd been, looking at a cliché, not Betty.

"It's great—the way you're looking at me. Yes, I have kids. Two little girls. My husband kept them when I fell in love with a woman and had to leave."

She was going to start confessing something. Why did this happen to me? Why did I attract the lonely, the miserable, the desperate—and why did they feel such a need to confide in me? I looked down at my letter to Iris.

Let's wake up here, Iris. Let's face the fact that *this is not* happening to you—at least not under hypnosis, kiddo. Who is it that you're inviting into your room at night?

Betty took another swig. "My husband won custody of the children when I left. He won't let me see them. He's convinced the court I'm a bad influence. He told me on the phone that the oldest thinks I'm dead."

She sat up and banged the vodka bottle on the desk. It splashed over the top and spritzed a few more letters.

"I'm not alive? Do I look dead to you? Don't I look like I'm still the mother of Jenna and Louise? It's Lou-Lou's birthday today; she's nine and I sent her a gift. I had a SIS messenger take it over to their apartment—my ex-husband told her to wait a minute, went out of the room, then came back with the gift and told the messenger to return it to me."

She flipped something across the desk. It was a package wrapped in red-and-blue paper with a bright red bow, a tiny plastic clown dancing from the bow. A piece of ruled writing paper had been taped to the package. On it was painstakingly printed:

LEAVE ME ALONE MOMMY. YOUR DEAD. FOREVER.

I handed the package back.

We sat in silence for a while, then Betty Berry stood up. "Jesus, Willis," she said. "When are you going to take those fucking rabbit ears off? You look like a goddamn idiot."

She picked up her bottle and her terrible package and shoved off, teetering a little. I stood up and walked, glancing at my reflection across the room in the opaque windows of late afternoon. An elongated, square-cornered figure in an antennalike headpiece slowed down, stopped to stare. I did look like a goddamn idiot.

I sat down, pulled off the rabbit ears, and tore up the soggy letter to Iris Moss. And began to type another.

Dear Iris,

I just destroyed a very smart-aleck letter to you written by me in a state of mind that had nothing to do with your communication to SIS. First of all, SIS can't pay

you for your thoughts; we don't accept unsolicited manuscripts. We *do* publish letters to the editor occasionally,
but I think your remarks might be misunderstood by
our general reading public. I'm presumptuous enough
to think I understand what you're talking about in your
letter. I am touched by your straightforward presenta-
tion of the facts of your life, including the hypnosis-
rapes you endure. There is a part of everyone's mind
that's hypnotized, that cannot look at itself. I have so
much in me that's in a trance, a state of suggestion. Iris,
I would like to stay in touch with you. I would like to
know if you ever discover the identity of this intruder-
in-sleep. I would like very much to know what is going
to happen to us.

Write soon,
WJD

Two

After supper and the dwindling campfire: unexpected rain. A huge rustle, an intimate downpouring, coming in fast over the tops of the trees. We stamped the fire into hanging smoke. "Good night, Dad," I called as the fathers went off. I lifted my red hunting cap and felt the drops, cold minnows, down the back of my neck.

We pushed each other into the tent, laughing and yelling, smudging matches till the kerosene lantern took, then turned odd gold faces to one another, the three boys and me. A long silence. Somebody popped bubble gum in fast snaps and sucking-in noises. The tent walls were sweating like skin and twitched at the pitch poles in the high wind, in the rifting piss-sound of rain.

I yawned. I took six green, gold, and brown mottled feathers from my pocket, turning them over in the light. Then I felt them all looking at me.

Sons of colonels, sons of officers, Army brats. Next to my olive-drab sleeping bag, my .22 lay in its case, much-prized Christmas present, predictable climax to a long gift history of fishing rods, baseball bats, boxing gloves. *"Willis my boy,"* he said.

"Willis. What kind of name is that for a girl? If she *is* a girl. She sure doesn't look like one." The big one threw these remarks over his shoulder to the others as he unrolled his sleeping bag. The others laughed nervously.

I pulled off the red hat, the braids unwinding to my shoulders, shrugging off drops like the retriever. *Now do I look like one?* I didn't have to speak. I unrolled my bag, fished some oily rags from beneath, picked up the .22 to clean it.

I'd shot six pheasants, blown them up as they broke cover, before the dogs pointed, before anyone had time to think. The act of killing interested me less than speculation on points of vulnerability in the field. Though I wouldn't have put it quite that way at eleven. I'd have said I liked to "sight," that I had an eye. What wished desperately not to move moved at last, had to move: The muscles of the heart expanded in the chest cavity, the delicate nerves of the wing twitched in fear. I didn't think about what happened after that. I had some kind of psychic spotter on the beating hearts and the aching wings in the brush. Then I stopped looking. I held my breath and pulled the trigger. Sure shot.

He had an Orange Crush bottle—it blazed in his hand in the lantern light. The rain started in harder. The littlest boy, Stevie MacAllister, shrieked in expectation. "Whaddya gonna do, Matthew, watcha doin'?"

Later I'd hear my mother's voice behind their bedroom door. "You let her sleep in a tent with the boys. What were you trying to prove? What did you think would happen?"

Maybe he was trying to prove once and for all that I was a boy; maybe he thought I'd beat them all up. Or he'd recognized that we'd both have to admit, finally, that I was a girl—after I took the worst of it. But what did he think I'd think, or feel, coming up against the inevitable in that tent?

"We're gonna play Spin the Bottle. We're all gonna play."

I laughed. "Which means that you guys get to kiss each other when it points to any of you."

Stevie, the little one, whooped in giddiness, then covered his mouth and peered at me, like a little Monkey Speak No Evil.

"No, *Willis*, you're wrong." He was a big, squat kid, Matthew, eleven or so, twelve. He was good looking, brown curls and labrador brown eyes, but his movements were jerky; he looked away from the things he talked to or touched.

He wasn't looking at me as he addressed me. "Nah, I think that Colonel Digby's daughter here will get kissed the most, because she's a girl, aren't you?"

I looked at him, but he wasn't looking at me—or the other boys either. He was blind, in himself. "I'm not *exactly* a girl," I said.

He didn't seem to hear. He set the bottle down, and when he took his hand away it seemed to begin turning in circles by itself, because he was not looking at what he was doing.

The second oldest, Danny, hung the lantern from a pole. The lantern began swinging to its own rhythm, switchblading light all over the tent. The pure lack of emphasis on Matthew's face drew light.

The bottle stopped, pointing directly at the tent flaps.

"Hey, Matthew?" I yelled. "Go out there and kiss a big fat grizzly bear. That's where it's pointing."

"Guess what?" He pursed his lips and made big wet kissing noises. "I get another turn, since it didn't designate anyone." The word "designate," an adult word, remained in the air.

I shivered and put the rifle aside. The bottle stopped at Stevie. I leaped in the air. "Hah—ahah—kiss away, Matthew Kissyface Smoochbird! Kiss that kid on the mouth! Woo-woo!"

I rolled around on the floor, shrieking with laughter, then

I sat up and applauded them both solemnly. I stuck the pheasant feathers in my braids and winked and wolf-whistled, a finger at each corner of my mouth.

"Let's go. Whaddya waiting for, you sly turtledovies, you. Hey, *let's go.*"

Matthew looked just over my head, his eyes glittering. "No. What it means for whoever's spinning the bottle is that if it stops at anyone other than you, that person gets to kiss you."

"Whaddya mean, Matthew? *That* means I *always* get kissed."

"That's right, *Willis.*"

"No, that's *wrong.*" I stood up. "I don't like this game. I'm not going to play anymore."

Matthew stood up too, pulling Stevie to his feet. "Yeah, you are."

I caught Danny's face in my peripheral vision; he was staring emotionless: the one who looks on. Then Stevie was in my arms. I fell backward with him. We looked terrified into each other's eyes. Then we looked up at Matthew.

"Kiss her."

Stevie made a terrible face.

"Kiss her."

"Get *off*, Stevie, you're hurting my foot."

"*Kiss* her."

Stevie looked at me in despair, brushed my lips with his. He smelled like Double Bubble.

"I mean *really* kiss her. Use your tongue."

Danny began to laugh. Horror crossed the face in front of me, then resignation, then inspiration. Stevie shut his eyes, stuck out his tongue and gave my face a long lick. I began laughing too.

Then it happened so fast. Stevie's body squirming away and Matthew, in a full leap, blocking out the light, landing on me. The two of us rolling over and over. Danny's expression floating somewhere: absolutely present, absolutely removed.

"Get off of me, or I'll beat you bloody, you stupid ugly jerk!"

"No. No way. I'm going to kiss you. *French* kiss you. Get it, you stupid girl, you *twat.*"

No. My whole body was a no. I knew I could put up a pretty good vicious fight, but I was having trouble getting started. I felt exhausted. I actually seemed to be falling asleep suddenly.

"Hey, wake up!" He shook me. Then I felt his hands prowling in the region of my breasts, or what I referred to as my breasts. They were small, but disproportionately important to me. I kicked; I bit into his neck; I slugged full force into his jaw.

"Ow. Okay, bitch."

We smashed at each other with our fists. I didn't care that he was bigger—his size seemed a distinct advantage to me in my anger; there was so much more of him to hurt. There was a tiny part of me still asleep, but the rest fought without any style or self-presence, no sense of pain. Something wet wobbled over my top lip into my teeth. Gradually I recognized the taste of blood.

A fight is an intensely private world. We were revolving somewhere far into space; the fathers couldn't have pulled us apart.

My mother's voice behind the door: "Who do you blame? That's right, drink some more, take another shot: I know who to blame."

But there was no blame for his hand, unstoppable, inching up my thigh. And my hand pulling, pumping wildly, a snapped wing. I knew what I had to protect—I knew what was violently new between my legs. What had begun in pain that morning, what I had stopped with a rag from my pack, taboo.

I spit blood in his eyes. He twisted my thigh, I pounded a fist three times into his ear before he screamed and smashed back, poking fingers in my eye.

We were both crying. One eye shut, I felt wildly on the floor for the bottle. His hand was nearly at the entrance, the opening to the center of me. My bloody teeth left red tracks up his arm; I noticed them as I felt for the bottle with my free hand: somewhere behind him, somewhere to the right. My hand struck something metallic, not glass—just as his hand moved into position, pushed apart my legs, triumphant, the fingers opening the cloth, the zipper.

I was using the gun as a club before I realized I had it in my hand, then I became aware of movement in the tent: Stevie screaming out into the night, Danny somehow close by, but at a distance, all eyes. I saw my arm lifting the rifle against the light—just as his hand entered me.

He did it in such a leisurely fashion, with one hand. He reached behind with the other, like stretching, pulled the rifle effortlessly out of my hand. I saw the butt coming down and tried to duck, but the blow stunned every muscle in my face and laid my head to the side, as he used the gun like a broom, sweeping my face.

Then everything stopped. He'd pulled his hand, bloody from my jeans, and when I got my eyes working I saw that he held his hand frozen, a few inches from his face, staring. The rifle was propped against his other arm.

He looked at me, for the first time, straight on. I pulled the gun away and he grabbed for it halfheartedly. He was looking at me. I could feel his heart expanding, pounding; his eyes were in mine, no longer distracted. And as the lazy tug-of-war started and we began to move, rolling over each other, his eyes stayed right there looking into me. And when it happened, when the gun went off, I remember his expression was not surprised, although the physical had betrayed him into a new fear and awe, a pure chivalric hate, I think now, as I hold that body again in my imagination, as it shakes and shakes, dying, and I at last put my lips to his, kissing him.

DEAR DIGBY

31

Three

Dear Letters Editor,

At present I am living in an aquarium. Several months ago I noticed that scales were beginning to grow on my arms, and I went to a dermatologist who told me, after he'd looked at them through a microscope, that he'd only seen scales like these before on a Red Snapper.

It wasn't long before the scales were all over my body and I started growing fins and a tail. Then I found that I had to put my head in the sink or soak it in the bathtub for hours. I was having lots of trouble breathing. One day I was at Crestwood Mall and I noticed an enormous wall-size aquarium in Pet World and I ordered one for myself. It's somewhat restrictive, but I float a lot and blow bubbles . . . the weirdest thing about all this is: My husband just stands there and stares at me through the glass. He stands for hours; he smokes cigarettes; he has a can of beer. Sometimes he puts his head up against the glass and says, "Georgette, Georgette, I'm so sorry. Georgie, I'm sorry, Georgie."

Carol Muske-Dukes

What I'm writing about, however, is this. I'd like to know if you would be interested in the story (firsthand account!) of a woman who has become a fish? I am out of the water enough each day to get it written down. I really feel that it is not your run-of-the-mill article. I worked at Macy's, in Notions, for several years if you think that would make a better story. (Also, I feel that I don't have much time because I am fairly certain that my husband is becoming a cat.) Please let me know as soon as possible. I am *not* a mermaid; I consider mermaids a sexist myth.

Sincerely,
Georgette Bell

I put the letter down and looked across to Page's desk, but she was busily typing, talking into a phone held under her chin. That was the trouble, you had to interrupt people and make them listen to these things; you had to break through their normal preoccupations and introduce this spiky stuff: wronged misogynists, women who thought they were turning into fish; a man who was king of New Jersey. "But hey," he wrote, "I'm a *fun* king." They began to associate you with the material, the interruptees; they associated you with the twisted scenery.

Minnie White-White-Goldfarb padded by and dropped another U.S. Mail bag next to my IN box. She smiled. She was happy again; she and her fiancé had each agreed to drop a name. I smiled back at her.

"More letters from loonies!" she sang.

I looked hopefully at the canvas mail sack. After my speech at the editorial meeting and my conversation with Betty Berry, I'd found it harder than I'd thought to find publishable letters from crazies. They were either like the one from Fish-Woman, a missile with a target so specific and mysterious it was irrelevant finally, not very funny—or they were hostile, offensive, frightening as a face in the window at midnight. I'd stopped wearing my rabbit ears, but I still felt oddly split—half the time I wanted to start a bonfire in my IN box and the other half I felt like one of them.

I upended the sack and shook out part of its contents. Blue envelopes, fuchsia, rainbow, a postcard from Sarasota Springs, Florida, fluttered free—then a postcard with a photo front. Somebody had taken a picture of Holly Partz at a rally; she stood at an outdoor podium under the trees, her long blond hair blowing, smiling into the mike, her arm raised in a feminist salute. Unfortunately, someone had inked a mustache and beard on her face and had crudely drawn what looked like a three-foot dildo in her upraised fist—on the back of the card was written, "SIS finally figures out how to use it!" in purple marker. Under the card was a sodden-looking package, I poked at it, afraid of plastique, or worse, home-cooked food. Then a letter fell free whose return address I recognized.

Iris had chosen to write to me this time on stationery sporting a recurring pattern of small chartreuse blimps with a large green leprechaun in the margin waving a flag that said, "Top of the Mornin' to Ya," on it.

Dear Mr. Digby [I realized that I had forgotten to tell her I was a woman.],

You're right. I think every woman goes through hypnosis-rape. I think every woman is not actualized to be the person she was meant to be. Just this morning, when I found seminal fluid leaking from my panties, I said to myself—*that's* how they keep women down, by violating their precious bodies! It's rape that keeps us in line. Or, more to the point, seminal fluid! Shouldn't we all think about this?

Carol Muske-Dukes

The letter went on, more about seminal fluid and violation, but I decided to cut it after the first paragraph and use it, without the "Mr." Digby. This, combined with a letter from a woman who got back at her husband (who refused to ever cook a meal for her) by secretly mixing Nine Lives cat food into his cereal every morning, and the letter from Dino Pedrelli and my answer—seemed to be the ticket. What a column!

I whistled a little. It was all coming together. I would try these letters on my readers as an introduction, then I would publish more and more in my column (as the demand rose) of the *unusual*, or I corrected myself, the usual unusual. Letters from the people who were not on the political barricades but had found other ways to deal with their frustrations. It would be fascinating. I could imagine the Letters column as a kind of human event, the soul of the magazine.

I proofread quickly, tagged the yellow sheets for publication, then turned my attention to the other correspondence, nearly *barking* in its impatience to be noticed. Now for the dailiness of my job, the task of teaching the lesson of official indifference—the job of slipping the Xeroxed brushoff in the SIS envelope, the job of typing the cute little letter of discouragement or downright bureaucratic censure, refusing the demands for publication, money, legal assistance, home phone numbers and addresses of staff, jobs at SIS or the White House, requests for photographs of editors, spiritual, physical, or psychic solace. Then the decisions re: bulk mail—what to do about the clods of foil-wrapped cheese from Wisconsin, the frozen merletons from Arcadia, the three and a half pounds of Liberated Chili from El Paso?

I had my seventh letter from the Pissed-Off Chef. She wanted SIS to help her "break into the TV Cook Show racket"—her signature music was going to be the sound of a frying pan smashing through window glass, a loud scream, then a snatch of Mahler's Resurrection Symphony. The

P.O.C. felt that there were a lot of women out there who hated to cook—and who had built up a lot of anger about cooking. Why these bon vivant, giggling-gourmet types? she demanded, ladling their strawberry soup and mincing basil, with no screaming kids or gerbils underfoot—and why old Julia with her ninety dirty dishes per recipe? She told me she could drop-kick a twenty-pound turkey about fifty yards—from the trunk of the car through the kitchen window and hit the roaster pan. She would *stomp* ingredients—as opposed to fileting, pounding, pestling. She could flatten five pounds of brisket into a slim patty with her big Spring-o-lator shoes and butterfly a pork butt wielding a double-bladed ax. She tested her linguine for readiness, *not* by flinging it lightly against a wall. She preferred lobbing fistfuls at a blown-up portrait of Wolfgang Puck.

I was sorely tempted to contribute a new recipe, which involved fish quenelles and Velcro snaps, but I restrained myself.

In fact, I tried heroically to remain neutral all morning, but *then*, then the old devil came over me—I had to write *personal* answers to some of the stuff. I took out my pen and added a few lines of suggestions about personal hygiene on the same page as the "official" answer to a particularly venomous male correspondent. I typed some of my own recipe hints for the woman who laced her hubby's Grape Nuts with Nine Lives. I took the rabbit ears out of my drawer and put them on.

I wrote to Iris again.

Dear Iris,

First, I really must mention to you that I am a woman, not a man. My father gave me a boy's name because he wanted a boy. I've never changed it; I've grown used to it—but it is often confusing and I apologize for this confusion.

Second, I would like to publish part of your recent letter to me in the Letters column. We do not pay for the right to publish letters, but I would personally like to thank you for the opportunity to print your opinions.

Have you made any progress in determining who your sleep intruder is? Since I've been Letters Editor here, I have the same sense (as I mentioned to you in an earlier letter) that alien brains are taking over my own thought processes.

Keep me posted about your progress in this important matter.

Yrs,
WJD

A paper clip hit me in the neck as I sealed the letter. I looked over at Page.

"You've got the *rabbit ears* on again, Willis. Take them off, they make me nervous about *who's* really across from me!"

I made a werewolf face at her, shrugged, and pulled out the rest of the mail from the sack. There was a medium-sized envelope with what looked like a bloodstain in the upper left-hand corner, and the initials W.I.T.C.H. hand-printed over the red stain. Trouble. I put the envelope down and stared at it. My name, on the face of the envelope, was put together from cutout letters. I flipped it over—there was a red wax seal with the symbol imprint, the bio-sign of the female with an eye inside. I opened the envelope, and a sheet of paper covered with cutout words fell out.

PRINT THE FOLLOWING.

Dear Letters Editor,
   W.I.T.C.H. (Women's International Terrorist Conspiracy from Hell) has a test for every SIS reader. It will allow you to rate your husband, boyfriend, lover, from 1 to 10. It will tell you if he is secretly sexist. Ask him the following questions.

On the flip side there were some typed questions under the heading SEXISM QUIZ.

1. You're on vacation; who would you rather have as a scuba-diving partner?
   A. Dolly Parton
   B. Sandra Day O'Connor

2. Let's say God is a woman. How would the world be different?
   A. Churches would have no steeples.
   B. The Pope would have PMS.
   C. Orthodox Jews would thank God every morning they were not born God.

3. Let's say your boss is a woman; would you prefer her to have:
   A. Big breasts
   B. Small breasts
   C. Trick buttocks
   D. Joan Crawford shoulders

4. Let's say you have prostate trouble. Would you prefer to visit a woman surgeon who looked like:

A. Madame Chiang Kai-shek
B. Pat Nixon
C. Tina Turner
D. Sylvester Stallone

At the end of the list of questions, W.I.T.C.H had this comment. "If your husband, lover, boyfriend has seriously tried to answer *any* of these questions, he is sexist to the bone. How could anyone with sensitivity to women even *listen* to these questions, ask yourself *that!*"

I stopped reading. Print this? Out of the corner of my eye, I saw Lupé Reyes glide by the drinking fountain. She gave me a high sign; her hand flashed in the sun and I saw the ring with its big inset stone: bio-sign, eye inside.

Lupé sidled over. She had on overalls, a bandana blouse, and a Walkman.

"Pretty funny, huh? You wanted to print some *extreme* stuff. We've got *more* tests for your public to take, after this one."

I must have looked horrified, because she chucked me under the chin, then winked. "It's all in *fun*, Willis," she said.

I smiled wanly at her. "It strikes me as a little *hostile*, you know?"

"You don't want to be *hostile*, do you, Willis?" She smiled back, her slow-developing smile, dug her finger into her temple and began to rapidly twist a long strand of dark curly hair. It looked like she was making the loco gesture at her own head.

We stared at each other for a while. The hair, revolving, set up an orbit of tension that multiplied outside the sliding partitions: Someone sharpened a pencil, someone wrapped a package, winding the twine around and around; a tangled phone cord, dangling, unwound faster and faster.

The hair stopped. "I don't know," Lupé said. "I don't

know about you, Digby. I mean, your sense of humor, I thought you were hip."

I narrowed my eyes and slouched a little in my chair: a honky editor trying to be hip. No luck. For years I'd applied an exotic rule of thumb that never failed me in determining instantly (in the right situation) if the woman I'd just met was destined to be a Real Friend. Could she sing "A Boy Like That" from *West Side Story*? I mean, really sing it, the way Rita Moreno did and whoever was the dubbed-in voice for Natalie Wood—with accusing postures, gestures, a heavy Puerto Rican accent—the whole bit?

A boy like that . . . will kill your brother.
Forget that boy and find another!
One of your own kind, stick to your own kind!

A boy who kills cannot love.
A boy who kills has no heart!
And he's the boy who gets your love,
And gets your heart . . . very smart, Maria, very smart!

Everybody knows "When You're a Jet" and "Dear Officer Krupke"—only a real purist, a certain kind of obsessive spirit, will have the duet by heart, the crackpot intertwining arias of Anita and Maria. Try it, it never fails. Still, though I felt a terrible urge to do so, I found that I could not launch into Anita's part, I mean really *do* the Spanish accent, with Lupé staring at me. Somehow, though I knew we liked each other, I doubted she would go with the flow here.

Lupé drew me back. "You're afraid of me, aren't you? You're afraid that I'm going to tell you some really horrible stories about myself, right?" She leaned closer. "Haven't you heard the one about my father pimping me?"

"I have."

"It's true."

"*Now* what am I supposed to say?"

"Hmmmmmm . . . what *should* you say? Do you think I oughta write a letter to you, give you a little more time to think up a response?" She threw back her head and laughed, then put her hand to her right cheek, let it slide slowly down, pulling the lower eyelid away from the eye.

"C'mon, Dear Abby, what advice do you have for *me*? My poppa dressed me up in a little see-through sundress with teddy bear pins holding up the straps, and he took me into the bars in East Harlem with his other girls. *Nueva carne,* they called me. Oh, look, do you think that's *awful?*"

She took my face in both hands and turned it around to look directly into her own.

"Does that make you feel bad? What if I wrote to you, Letters Editor, about my awful, awful father, huh? Or what if I wrote you about my sister, the one he liked to rape— she began to hear *voices,* but no, it was *funny,* the voices told her to shit in his shoes and sew his pants shut—you like that kind of thing, don't you?" She dropped her hands.

"She sewed his pants shut?"

"Yeah. Then he came raging after her and stepped into his shoes, which were full of shit."

I laughed.

"You see? It *is* funny—you're right! Think about this, everybody at the Women's House was a laugh riot. You know, either in for boosting Kotex or blowing their old man's head off—nothing in between! No armed robbery, no break-ins. And everybody inside signed up for Serena de Villa-neuve Charm School. I did too—we all wanted the free Ice Blue Secret. Some wanted to smell better and some smashed the little rolling glass balls and made slicers to protect their jailhouse lovers. Corrections freaked out, they hadn't thought ahead. They *never* found all those little bits of glass— those with B.O. fought harder to hide the stuff than the weapon makers. They once called a hunger strike protesting the fact that they were not allowed to see an Avon Lady. I *swear* to you. Women try to be happy at any cost. They have their own justice. They're *crazy*, women, that's why W.I.T.C.H. can save the fuckin' world, Digby."

"I don't even know what W.I.T.C.H. is."

"Your loss. For me, it was W.I.T.C.H. or Felony One. It's something between jostling and blowing Daddy's brains out." She touched the W.I.T.C.H. ring on her finger. "I gotta tell you, if ever anybody in my experience needed W.I.T.C.H., my friend, I'd say you do. Something's after you."

I did listen to what she said; I thought about it. I could feel the dark around her, not a threatening dark, but a night-town badger-black inventiveness. Tricks that keep you sane.

That night after work I saw the shopping bag lady again, the same sunburned crone I always saw at the corner. I tried to avoid her, but she followed me, singling me out. She puffed and shuffled right in front of me, poking her wizened tortoise face into mine. Her eyebrows bristled like a scholar's.

"Ed Koch was down here again, sniffing bicycle seats. I got proof!"

"Listen, I don't feel too well," I said. I gave her a dollar.

"You're so cheap you squeak. You know what I mean, dipshit?" She hawked and spit sideways at a passerby. He scowled at both of us and brushed at his overcoat.

I gave her a five. She checked to see if it was a counterfeit, licked it, then stuffed it in her sock.

"Hey—don't walk so fast—there's somethin' *wrong* with you! A bad disease, girlie. I call it Psycho Blood."

I gave her another five. I had no more cash. She licked and stashed it, then rattled after me, yelling, "You look like a ghost. Getta tranfusion, dipshit!"

I turned in at the subway entrance and ran down the steps.

"GETTA TRANSFUSION IN YOUR HEAD!" she yelled

after me. I could hear her repeating it, screeching into the subway well. "A TRANSFUSION, DIPSHIT!"

I got on the local and felt another darkness seep into me. Like a transfusion: wrong blood type.

When I got home, I stretched out in the tub with my clothes on (a technique that never fails to relax me) and puffed on a joint.

Lupé and the shopping bag lady had been bad enough, but the worst part of my day, the real bottom-out, was a letter, one among hundreds in the morning mail. I pulled it out of my pocket.

I'm writing to you because I'm depressed, and I keep thinking that if I write down how I feel, it will help. I lost my baby a year ago today. I miscarried at six months—he just came too early. His name was Patrick. The doctors don't want me to get pregnant again—there were some complications. I don't want to get pregnant again, either. You see, I want Patrick. Can you believe that I'm sitting in the room that was supposed to be his nursery? It's 3 A.M., I'm all alone in here—they've taken out the bassinet and toys—but it's still white and empty and *expectant*, it's still a nursery waiting for a child. The thing I wanted to tell you was that I *talk* to Patrick when I'm alone like this, in the house, or when I'm driving in the car. I sing him songs, nursery rhymes. I tell him how I feel, I tell him what kind of day it's been. This is the only comfort I have in the world right now—all the rest of it, my home and my husband, mean so little. You see, I saw him through glass. I got out of bed against orders and got down to the Newborn Intensive Care Unit. I saw him mothered by a robot, all the tubes running in and out of him and the respirator pumping his lungs. I screamed and fought, but they would not let me hold him. They wouldn't even let him die in my arms when *that* time came. I hit a nurse so hard they had to resuscitate her. My husband told me later he thought I'd lost my mind, he told me he was mortified by the way I acted. I tell you I could have smashed through that glass wall with my bare fists, and I *should* have, I should have smashed them all out of the way, and held him in my arms—but they got me, they stuck a needle in me and sedated me. Now my husband and my mother have decided I need therapy—because they found out I talk to Patrick. Will I go? *Yes*, because they'll make me. Will I give up Patrick? *No, never.* I will kill myself first. I have a gun. I have pills. Please understand—I'm sorry about this letter. I don't know you, but I just had to write this down, write it to *someone.* If they take Patrick from me now, it will be the end.

Tracy St. Martin

Erie, Pennsylvania

I slid down in the tub and inhaled, staring up at the ceiling, up at the ersatz Tiffany lamp casting its stained-glass shadows on the Sistine-ceiling cracks.

Then I polished off the roach fast and pulled myself out of the tub. I hurried (before I could change my mind) across the living room to the telephone, found the area code for Erie, Pennsylvania, and got long-distance information and a number for an Allan St. Martin on Tamarack Street in Erie. I dialed the number.

A young woman's voice, very tentative, answered on the third ring.

"Hello," I said quickly. "This is Willis Digby from SIS magazine."

"What?" she said. "SIS?" Then there was such a long

silence, torn by quick, vicious rips of static, that I thought she'd hung up.

"Hello?" I called into the night.

"Yes?"

"Is this Tracy St. Martin—the one who wrote me the letter?"

Another long silence.

"Yes. This is Tracy."

"Tracy . . ." I glanced at the mirror on the wall, then away, fast, shocked at my wild, semistoned face.

"Hello?" she said.

"Tracy, I'm calling because I got your letter. . . . I just wanted to tell you that I'm so sorry about . . . Patrick."

"Oh, *God*," she said. The anguish in her voice cut through me. "Patrick." Then: "Is this a joke? You think this whole thing is a joke, don't you?"

"No," I said, "*no*. I do not. That's why I'm calling you up like this. I just wanted to let you know that even if you go to therapy, I think you can hang on to Patrick, you don't have to let him go. *Don't* let him go, *fuck 'em all! Excuse* me," I said. "I didn't mean that last comment."

"It's okay," she said. It sounded like she'd begun crying very softly.

"Just don't kill yourself. You see, that *would* be a bad joke. That wouldn't make sense here."

"Why?" She began sobbing outright. "*Why* is that?"

"Because . . ." I was sweating. *God, give me a reason fast,* I prayed—I looked at the mirror again, then away. "Because, *granted,* though it's a terrible life, one of its few bittersweet rewards is *foiling* people. I'm not going to give you any of that 'gaze at a grain of sand' shit. On the other hand, think of the personal satisfaction you might derive from *not* letting certain jerks you know stand around at your wake sipping sherry and saying, 'I told you so.' I mean, stuff like 'She was a lovely girl, but she just couldn't *take it;* after the baby's

. . . tragedy, she just went downhill, she folded up like—a little toy fan.' "

More silence. "Yeah?"

"Yeah. I mean, listen, Tracy. I know this comes across odd now, but it sounds to me like you'd rather bump off your husband and your mother than yourself."

Amazing. I heard laughter. Another sob. Then more laughter, higher pitched.

"If I were you, I'd *flaunt* my grief for a while. I'd talk to Patrick wherever and whenever I wanted to—let *them* back off for a while. Try to love your craziness while it lasts, you know? Personally, I think we should all have a Holy Crazy Lady we pray to. To save us. I even have one in mind."

"What is she like?"

"She's . . . *unusual*. Like Mary Poppins on the skids. You know, twenty years later with the shakes, no teeth, and a fright wig. Trying to fly up with her umbrella, but ramming into buses, getting caught in power lines. Poking meter maids in the eye with her umbrella. You know the type. Or *I* do. Spoonful of acetylene."

Tracy was laughing softly and sniffling. "This is so *weird*," she said. "I work part-time as a manicurist and I thought I'd heard *everything* there was to hear. I'm *amazed* you called me—I'm amazed you even read my letter." I heard her blowing her nose, a discreet little honk.

"Of *course* I read your letter. I read every letter personally. SIS stands for nothing if not *sys*tematic," I squawked, shameless. There was another blast of static. "Besides," I continued when our connection kicked in, "I *know* how you feel. I . . . ."

"I believe I've heard *enough!*"

A male voice, nasal and twangy, *very* irritated, split our airwaves.

"Allan!" I heard her gasp. "How long have you been *on?*"

"I picked up at the beginning of this . . . *crank call*. I heard *everything*, Tracy. Including the bit about you writing to SIS magazine!"

She gasped again.

"Listen, Allan—" I began.

"*No. You* listen to *me.* You think you can call up my wife and tell her she secretly wants to *murder* her mother and me? Or that she should *flaunt* her *craziness*??? Who the hell are you? I'll *sue* your ass!"

"Allan," I said, "you sound exactly like Jerry Lewis! Has anyone ever told you that? Your voice has certain subtle intonations—like a drive-in speaker! But I'll try to overcome that impression! Let's be reasonable—did it ever occur to you that *eavesdropping* is creepy and wrong? Violates privacy? Or, even more to the point, that Tracy doesn't need you to make her feel guilty and crazy right now?"

"*Yeah*," said Tracy, "she's *right.*"

"Get off this phone and out of our lives!" he roared. "What about *my* privacy?"

"Stop talking to her like that," said Tracy. "I don't like it, Allan."

"Tracy, hang up."

"*No. You* hang up!"

"Well," I said, "that seems to make a majority here for flushing *Allan.* If you ask me . . ."

"*No one* asked you. I'll tell you what *I'm* going to do. I'm going to hang up this phone and come downstairs, Tracy, and hang yours up too. And then we're going to turn the phones off for tonight—we're going to forget about hearing from this maniac. Forever. And if she calls back tomorrow, I'm calling the police. Do I make myself understood?"

He didn't wait for our answers—I heard a determined click.

"Miss Digby, I guess we have to say good-bye now. Thank you so much for calling me up tonight. I feel kind of . . . better. You're a very . . . *unusual* person."

"Thanks, Tracy. I'm feeling a bit perkier too. Like I was saying, I know pretty much what you've been going . . ."

The sound of arguing voices, then: "Allan, don't do that, don't hang up—Allan, you *jerk!*"

Then just static again, broken connection—and I was left alone again with my strange, familiar interlocutor, the night. And those other voices, the ones I've come to welcome and trust, the ones who talk to me, soothe me, cajole me, get me through to dawn.

"Lily?" I called. "Lily?" And Lily was *there*. She told me she'd listened to everything and she loved me. Lily would always love me.

Three days later, Minnie W-W-G hustled over with a registered special-delivery letter for which I had to sign. It was from Iris Moss.

Well, well, well, *Willis.*

So you are a *woman!* Ha! I say, *ha!* The reason I say "ha" is because I have come to the conclusion that my hypnotic-rapist may not be of male persuasion at all, but rather a *female.* These stains (which I found yet again this morning) may not be semen on my panties, but rather gynecological *juice* from the she-bitch in heat (excuse my profanity) who gets into my undergarments as I sleep and licks me, rolling her tongue over my cringing clitoris in passionate whorls of lust!

I have decided it is *a woman dressed as a man* who sneaks into my room. I see the whole sordid picture. I see that it is not semen that has been pumped into my vagina, it is your own female sexual arousal juices, your lubricants that facilitate sexual congress. You seem to me the type of person who would pursue vibrators and dildos, and in public places.

Editor of Letters, indeed! I spoke to my friend Basil Schrantz (a gentle man who wants nothing more than to be an Oral Surgeon), and he informed me that he is aware how you gain access to my room at night dressed as a man. He insists on remaining in my room, as I sleep, to protect me. So BEWARE! You will have to contend with Basil Schrantz if you plan to continue your frenzied tonguings of my labia major and minor.

I will write again, with details. Do not forget: I am *on* to you! I can have photographs taken! DO NOT PRINT THIS LETTER. Do not print my other letter to you either—I do not authorize it. If you do, I will sue you! (Or charge my professional writer's fee, which is $625.)

Do not try to contact me by telephone. I know how you are capable of sending germs (or worse) through the wires.

Utterly Disagreeing,
Iris L. Moss

Iris Moss's first letter had already been sent to the printer. I picked up my pen.

Dear Iris,

Basil Schrantz is wrong. I *do* dress as a man occasionally—but I don't fancy unconscious sex partners. Have you noticed Basil dressing up in female garb ever? Most specifically as a nurse?

Listen, Iris, let's not be enemies. I have this sense of you and me: that we can somehow help each other. I would like to continue to write to you. I like the thought of writing to a woman who's such a *fighter*, at least during waking hours.

I repeat, with regret, I cannot *pay* you for your thoughts. Your first letter has already gone to press; I promise this most recent one will not be published.

Sincerely,
WJD

The phone on my desk rang.

"Willis Digby here."

"Hey. Are you the crackpot there who sent me this smart-ass letter?"

"Who is this?"

"This is Dino Pedrelli. I wrote you frustrated old maids a letter about three weeks ago, and here I get this poison pen response that's tellin' me I'm *impotent*."

He said im-poh-tent. I remembered the letter suddenly. Dino the Dong.

"Yeah. So what do you want from me now? A balloon?"

There was a choking sound on the other end.

"Jesus. God. A man goes to work, he picks up a magazine to read on the subway, and he sees all this vicious crap"— he choked again—"he takes the time to write in, to *write in* to you bitches—and this is the thanks he gets? Tellin' me I'm im-po-tent?"

I hung up after Dino described in detail a few of his most recent sexual encounters, after he wept badly, after he'd promised me he would "make me pay" for this transgression.

"Guess what?" I called across to Page when I'd hung up. "Dino Pedrelli is *not* im-poh-tent."

She frowned and went back to her typewriter. "*Im*potent, Willis, *im*potent," she corrected.

Carol Muske-Dukes

50

Four

Get back, the voice was screaming through the bullhorn. *Get back, lie down, keep your eyes and mouth covered. Lie flat, cover your eyes!*

The crowd was stumbling and screaming, a single blinded animal. The tear gas hung in sick orange streamers in the 90-degree air. The police, in their riot gear, kept on coming. I felt a leather hand on my neck—it picked me up by my T-shirt the way a kitten is plucked up by the ruff. I wrenched around to get a look at my manipulator—and got a nightstick flat across the face. I saw the cop's face—big nose, helmet, mail-slot mouth—in a kind of 3-D ripple: green, red, then, mercifully, black.

When I came to, I heard someone screaming. I sincerely hoped that it would not turn out to be me. Nothing worse than catching yourself in a cliché. As it turned out, it wasn't me, but a fat Mamma-Cass-like woman nearby who had just caught a glimpse of my face. "Look at *that,* I'm going to faint!" she bellowed to someone. "Look at what happened to that poor girl!"

Someone else began pressing a cold wet cloth against my

nose. I brushed the cloth away and stared up into a blond, sympathetic moon-face. "Ah'm jus' tryin' to hep," she said.

I tried to retort but found that my lips and tongue seemed sealed together by a powerful mortar. I spit some blood on the grass.

"I think it's broken," I said, or *thought* I said, pointing to my nose.

The girl looked mystified. "Come ag'in?"

I wrestled my bruised tongue once more into speaking position.

"B'oken. My noth. My *noth!*" I shouted, losing patience, jabbing my finger at my proboscis.

The girl smiled beatifically and nodded, adjusting her white armband with the red cross, preparing to move off through the crowd, or what remained of it.

"Ah'm up heah from Alabama with a blues group. Ah'm jus' tryin' to he'p out."

She floated off, and I sat up, looked out over Pennsylvania Avenue. The crowd had been effectively dispersed, except for a few bloody hangers-on, like me, a few last-worders. Twenty minutes or so before, ten thousand people with banners reading: OUT OF VIETNAM NOW, STOP THE BOMBINGS, HO, HO, HO CHI MINH: VIET CONG'S GOING TO WIN, and WITHDRAW DICK had been milling in front of the White House, chanting, snake-dancing, smoking dope, waving their placards.

We had all come down to 1600 Pennsylvania Avenue to protest a brunch meeting that sat President Nixon down with the Joint Chiefs of Staff and some of the Vietnam Hawk generals, including Westmoreland. They were planning more bombings, as everyone knew; the meeting was obviously not a high-level strategy discussion—*those* were never witnessed—but their arrogance in coming together in such an upfront manner, with such public disregard of the nation's mood about recent war developments, had triggered this spontaneous demonstration in front of the White House—and as far as possible, or accessible, the White House lawn.

I had been in the vanguard of the Lawn Streakers—Rennie Meyer, my boyfriend (long since vanished), and several other friends and I had all joined hands, singing "Give Peace a Chance," waving Cong flags, and waltzed onto the grounds. All of the friends had disappeared, driven off in the front-line fire.

Holding a tissue gingerly to my nose, I searched for a familiar face. And suddenly, in the most unlikely of all places, I saw one. I can't remember the words that began flowing out of my mouth, but I began to cry out—and I began to run faster than I had ever run before in my life, through the impossible heat and the leftover gas, in the direction of the White House gates.

The generals, having finished their meeting with Nixon, had decided to board their limousines at the east gate, where they would also answer one or two fast questions from the press, then hop into their stretch Caddies. They apparently wanted to appear Calm and Steadfast for the media, in the midst of the morning's massacre.

As I ran toward them, they completed their cheery "No Comments" to the TV cameras, shook hands all around, began slithering into their shiny black hearses. I recognized Westmoreland, a couple of Joint Chiefs, but the first face I'd recognized was the one I was headed for.

No one saw me, no one tried to stop me, which was astounding, considering my physical appearance. The cops were scattered, everyone was intent on the circle of cameras and lights.

As I got within earshot, I began to shriek over my bloody lisp. "Colonel Digby!" I screamed. "Hey, I should say General Digby—I heard it on the news yesterday, General, General Digby?"

He whirled around and faced me—I was within three feet of him—and gasped. I must have looked like a ghoul from a basement horror flick: blood had coagulated, *crusted* on my face, hair, T-shirt, teeth. There was so much dried blood in my throat I was having trouble gettings words out.

"How do you like the way I look, Dad? *This* is what happens to people who want peace in this country! How do you like it, Dad? *How do you like it*—take a good look!"

I pushed in closer. His face was still handsome under his white hair, a *shocked* handsome face. He put up a hand as if to protect himself.

"Willis," he said. "What . . ."

Suddenly more leather hands were on my back; this time I could feel they Meant Business. He seemed about to protest, but then I bent, coughed, shook off the hands, stood up, and spit blood in his face.

"Killer," I screamed as they dragged me off. "Killer!"

After his telephone call, which came the next day, I left the doctor's office and stopped by my apartment to change before going to see him.

Consequently, I, Willis Jane Digby, am the only United States citizen who has ever walked into the offices of the Pentagon wearing bell-bottom jeans, no bra, a T-shirt reading FUCK THE WAR on both sides, a huge LEGALIZE MARIJUANA button, pink heart-shaped aviator glasses over my taped nose, a Janis Joplin hairdo, a necklace made of roach clips, and a fettuccine of bandages.

The guard who accompanied me to General D's office remained poker-faced, but I could feel his sidelong glances every now and again.

"Care for a cigarette?" I asked him—my jaw ached tremendously but somehow moving it helped.

He shook his head. "No, *ma'am*."

We entered General Digby's temporary office. He would

be shipping out in three days, they'd said on the news. I did not know the specifics of his commission.

We had not spoken in three years. Since I had gotten so involved with antiwar politics on campus, I found it impossible to communicate anything to him other than the shame I felt at his holding a position of such significance in this war. For his part, he remained fairly withdrawn; he offered little in the way of explanations.

I had come to see him today, when he called me, before he left for Vietnam, because I thought he might try to explain. As passionately as I believed that there was no explanation or forgiveness—a part of me wanted to hear my father (the way he had when I was a little girl) deliver a few choice words that clarified everything. Or maybe I just wanted another chance to say more about my own anger. Or maybe, I thought as I saw him standing up behind his desk—thin, tall, and powerful in his uniform—maybe I just wanted to see *him.*

To say good-bye.

We stood facing each other.

"That's an interesting outfit," he said. "You look like the antiwar celebrity you've become. I saw you spitting on me on all three channels on the six o'clock *and* the eleven o'clock news."

"Yeah, I'm a real star. Too bad I had to get my nose broken and my jaw slightly realigned in order to do it."

"Sit down, Willis."

I noticed a slight unsteadiness. Had he been sipping a bit?

"Yes, yes, I've had a drink," he answered, as if I'd asked the question out loud. "Would you like something? Scotch? Mixed drink? Wine?"

"No, thanks. Still hitting the sauce, huh?" I rearranged my button so that a FUCK THE WAR emblem caught a shaft of cool white light from his desk.

"Willis," he said, pouring a straight Scotch, "I admire you for putting yourself on the line like this, for getting your head bashed in because you care so much about protesting this war. However, you don't know shinola about what I'm trying to do—and while I would never expect you to admire me, I would ask that you reserve judgment of me."

Much to my horror, I found myself starting to cry, losing a breath as the tears stung the swollen flesh around my nose. "Wait a minute . . . waaaait a minute . . . *shinola*. Is *that* the stuff you guys use to shine your boots with? *Shinola*. Is that the stuff that burns the skin off little kids' faces—or eats up the grass and the trees? Yeah, I know that stuff. This is the Shinola War, isn't it?"

He laughed and took a drink and looked away. "You're proud of that mouth, aren't you?" he said.

He turned around suddenly and faced me, terrifying and quiet.

"Contrary to what you believe, there *is* an organized program of withdrawal. I'm going over there to assist that movement *out*. However, it's going to take time; patience—a virtue that you've never cultivated—is required."

"How can you sit there and lie like that?" I stood up, accidentally nudging my jaw and winced. "You know as well as I do that all we have to do to end this war is to *get out*."

"Willis, wake up. There's an entire population of Vietnamese who are now dependent on us. What's going to happen to those people if we turn tail and pull out? Anything good, do you think? Mass executions, petty dictators are just the—"

"I'm going now. I don't know what I came here for, but it certainly wasn't to hear a lecture on the U.S. global conscience. That's what started this whole thing."

"Willis," he said more insistently, "you do what you believe. I'm doing the same thing. How the hell can I help what you think of me? But I'm doing the only thing we *can* do over there. I wouldn't mind if you got that straight."

"Good-bye, General." I started to walk out and then something made me stop and turn around. He had his head bowed, his hand over his eyes.

I found myself walking toward him. I paused at the edge of his desk.

"The gun just went off that night," I said. I started to cry. "We were rolling around on the floor and then the gun went off . . . and Matthew Kallam was dead."

I was crying harder now. "It wasn't my fault. The gun just went off. *Why* did you leave me in that tent? Why?"

He kept looking down. "I raised you to be fearless, Willis— and you are, I think." He looked up at me. "You are. But being a woman and fearless"—he shook his head, troubled, and took a drink—"men will back away from you for that. I wasn't wrong to make you strong, was I? I was wrong not to tell you that men fear fearless women. How about a little mercy, Willis, how about a little mercy?"

I stood still, shaking. The room was perfectly silent. I reached over the desk and touched his cuff. "Good-bye, Father."

He touched my hand.

Six weeks later he was dead of a heart attack in Da Nang. They flew the body back, and at the funeral, after the rifle salute, when they took the flag from the casket, as it lowered, and folded it and placed it in my mother's hands, I wept with the others. And I stayed by the grave a long time, weeping.

For my father.

For my country.

For me, fearless Willis Digby. His son.

Five

Minnie W-W-G buzzed me on the intercom. "Someone here to see you at the front desk, Digby."

"Well, who is it?" I buzzed back testily. Ever since Minnie had settled her hyphenation problems, she'd been fabulously inefficient on the job—leafing through *Vogue*, sucking on low-fat yogurt pops, endlessly doing her nails.

"Ummmmmmm—jussasec, I'll check."

I was a bit cautious about whom I "saw" in Reception. Since I'd begun answering the more imaginative letters, I'd gotten a few visitors. One was a guy who insisted on meeting me because (he said) he'd had my handwriting analyzed and had been told by the graphologist that I was "multi-orgasmic," and he wanted to date me. Also, Dino Pedrelli had stopped by a few times, asking for me. I did *not* want to powwow with that gentleman either.

"Well?" I buzzed again.

Minnie fumbled back on. "She says her name is Moose. No, no. *Moss, Iris Moss.*"

"Just a second, I'll get right back to you."

Now what? Jesus, what if she had a gun, or worse? The possibilities of how Iris Moss might stock a personal arsenal were paralyzing to consider. What if she wanted to blow up SIS? I mean, she *did* think that I was entering her sleep under false pretenses. She was obviously here on a *mission*. I looked over at Holly's office. She was just coming out, brushing her hair out of her eyes, deep in conversation with Marge Taggart. She looked up and waved. I had told her we needed to talk to these crazy women—I had defended their right to be weird, or worse. I *had* to go out and face Iris Moss.

I approached Minnie's Reception platform (which had a bulletproof bubble she could raise and lower at will)—I wondered momentarily if I could get her to activate it and then let me address Iris on the microphone. I heard animated conversation.

" . . . and then I realized that liquid protein is *not* the answer and is so much less satisfying in terms of food image than even, say, cottage cheese and celery—or yogurt and bran. I mean, those are *boring* foods, but liquid protein is *unconscious* food, the kind of food you'd eat if you were a *chair.*"

Before Iris spoke, I looked at Minnie. Then I remembered—she'd decided to switch from glasses to contact lenses. She was on a big prewedding physical "make-over" kick—and just that morning she'd had drops put in her eyes at the ophthalmologist's office for the contact lens test. She was, for all practical visual purposes (like seeing the nose in front of her face) *blind.* She was working the switchboard by rote.

"Yes, yes: I know what you mean. At the hos—where I live, we seem to end up with a lot of starchy foods. I've gotten very strict about the way I eat. . . ." A high, oddly fluted voice, with a pronounced speech impediment, she swallowed her "P's" and "R's"; she said "stalchy", "stlict").

"I usually cut all the gristle off my pork chop, and I pick all the raisins out of everything: carrot salad, bran flakes, even ham sauce."

"Raisins are fattening?"

"Oh, I have no idea about that. I just don't like the way they *look*. If you think about it, they're very disgusting looking; they look like something that *died*, they *are* something that died—they look like the testicles of a chipmunk who's been stiff for a few days."

I could hear Minnie shifting in her seat at this observation. "Yeah," she said slowly. "I see your point."

There was a silence. Mercifully, the phones all began to ring at once. Lights flashed. Minnie went to work.

"SIS magazine . . . Hold the line please."

"SIS magazine . . . Same to you, buddy."

"SIS magazine . . . No, you want S.O.S. magazine—the psychology self-help quarterly, not *SIS*."

I stepped out into the garish light of Reception.

"Hello, Iris?" I put out my hand blindly. My hand closed over hard plastic, a ridged set of fingers. I flinched and jumped back, but the rigid plastic fingers held my hand in a crushing grip—I felt myself being pulled forward slowly by that pressure, and I looked straight into her eyes. She looked like an egg, a darning egg filled with sawdust; she looked stitched together. The hand she gripped mine with was a flesh-colored prosthetic device: five fingers, a hand, a forearm. She was wearing a sort of baggy tunic with elbow-length sleeves, into which the false arm vanished. Her forehead was x'ed with crisscrossed stitches, scars, and her eyes stared out from under shaggy unplucked brows from two different levels: a Picasso face, a Cubist Baseball. Her skin had the texture (and in places, the color) of a strawberry; the nose was broken and rebroken, the mouth a jagged tear, a ripped tin can lid. Her hair was a machine-made, marble-cake Afro, a Supreme's wig hat.

"Willis Digby?" she hissed through her sheared labial flap. *"Willis Jane Digby?"* She had pulled me so close to her that I could feel her breath on my face—it was oddly sweet, babylike, milk-breath. One of the eyes jumped and popped nearly out of its socket, gazing sideways at me.

"I am Iris Moss. Iris Luckley Moss."

The prosthetic fingers were digging into my flesh. I couldn't breathe or speak.

"Nerf," I gasped.

"What?" She poked one eye very close. "What did you say?"

"Nervous, I'm a bit ner-vous about meeting you finally." I pulled my face back from hers—we were locked in a frozen minuet—she pulling me toward her, my entire body retracting, drawing back.

At last she released my hand, which dropped to my side, bloodless. I put the other hand against the wall to steady myself. This was it—here before me was Horror, Inc. She was a real, breathing, conversing *monster.* A monster. I saw my corpse laid out on the shag carpet at my feet, huge claw marks across my face.

"Minnie," I called hoarsely, realizing even as I called that it was barely a croak and that Minnie, engrossed in the phones, was cheerfully sightless. "Minnie—" I tried again, but what issued from my throat was that sound we all make, midnightmare, somewhere between a growl and a silent scream.

From the folds of her tunic, beneath which I could see a tropical shirt with interlocking banjos and plam trees and "Laupahoehoe, Hawaii" in wavy script, she brought forth (with a pinch of the prosthetic fingers) a pair of extra-large-size elastic-band women's underpants. They were patterned with large blue roses.

"See these?"

"Uhhhh-yeah. Those are . . . ah . . . underpants."

"Yes, underpants." The pop-eyes swiveled about the room and found a half-lit corner.

"Sit down over there. *Sit*," she repeated, and pushed me into the wings with the false arm.

I dropped down on the couch like a P.O.W., cringing and grinning hysterically.

She sat down, pushed her face close again.

"Willis Digby . . . these are my underpants here, a pair of my underpants. And do you know what they're stained with?" She shook the underpants up and down.

"Eeeep."

"Eeeep?"

"No. No. Agh . . . seminal fluid?"

"That's right! That's correct, Willis Digby! These underpants, my *private* things, are stained with *seminal fluid*. Now. Do you know what this is?"

"Heeerp-o-dermic needle?"

"Yes. This is a hypodermic needle. Do you know what a needle like this is used for?"

I gasped.

"What?"

"Uh—a syringe? To introduce medication intravenously? For pain or sleep?" I tried to look stern, medical. Maybe if I reminded her of a nurse she'd become docile, passive. What *was* that huge needle for? I shuddered.

She nodded cautiously. "Yes. Sleep medication. Basil Schrantz did it. He introduced sleep medication into me every night and then used me for his unspeakable, seminal purposes! His job was just to give out the pills at night—I didn't know that. I thought he was *supposed* to give me that hypo. He told me it was vitamin serum. He was an *orderly!*" she shrieked, and the arm shot up by itself, spread into a claw. She got it under control in the nick of time, then pointed one of the fingers at me.

"I trusted him. But he was no orderly, he was *disorderly* by night. But you, Willis, you were right. You put me on to him in your letter to me . . . and I can't thank you enough." The hand fluttered to rest on my knee. Relief flooded through my body.

"He would come in, pretending to give me a little goodnight pill, and then take out this *spike*, which he had appropriated from Third Floor Diagnostic. He'd stick two hundred cc's of chloral hydrate into my arm, and then . . . and then . . ."

The fingers clutched my knee.

"Seminal fluid!" I cried, like a cheerleader.

"Yes. Seminal fluid. I found it in the morning, every morning in my panties. But I just *never* thought it could be Basil. He was my *friend*."

The eyes rolled pathetically, and instantly I felt it. What it must be like to live inside that body—to have to distrust every reaction: the false pity, the horror, the embarrassment—till the eyes of the possible friend could see beyond the sutured flesh, the crooked eyes, the ripped mouth.

"Jesus. Will anyone prosecute? Isn't this a scandal for the state? I mean, for your place of residence?"

"For Brookheart State Hospital—yes. It's a *shame*, but it will never be a scandal—not if they can help it. They just want it hushed up. They fired Basil Schrantz, of course—then they asked me for the needle—but I wouldn't give it to them. I know what happens to important evidence when they get hold of it. They *say* they're going to hold it for the official investigation—and then, mysteriously, it *disappears*! Just like that." She actually snapped two of the plastic fingers—the sound was like a beaded curtain shaking.

"Therefore"—she rolled the syringe back up in a piece of cheesecloth—"I'm keeping it for myself. Keeping the fingerprints fresh—for the FBI—or the president."

I couldn't help myself; I *had* to wonder how much of all this was true. "How did you get . . . When did you arrive here?

"I just *left* the hospital. It's easy enough to do. There are guards, but they're not very smart. The grounds have no real fences or barred gates."

An eye cocked at me. "Do you doubt my story, Willis?"

"Oh, *no*. No. I just wondered how you managed to get down here so quickly."

"Train. God told me to take the train. She said, 'Iris, take the train to SIS.' "

"Sure," I said. "Sure, He *would*. He never cared much about transportation."

"And now I can thank you *face to face*."

"You're welcome. But you did it all yourself, it's your story. And . . . after this . . . what are your plans?"

What if she wants to stay here, to work here, to see me every day?

"To go back to Brookheart, of course. *I love it there*," she said, with a little frown of surprise. "I'm *crazy*. I'll go now, now that I've met you and spoken to you."

"Well, thank you. I meant what I said in the letter, I'd like to keep in touch, Iris. I feel there's a reason for us to be regular correspondents, you know?"

"Yes . . . I think so. We do have similarities. I mean, finally I believe that all this happened to me because of my looks."

I stared at her. Poor woman. Jesus, were there weirdos in this world who *specialized* in Ugly Love, who preyed on the deformed?

"Yeah?"

"Oh, yes. A woman of my looks has to be very careful. I mean, I almost don't blame Basil Schrantz, as horrible as all this is, for falling for me like that; it happens to me all the time. At first I was going to kill him—as I said in the letter, it would have given me *great* satisfaction. In fact, I was standing over him with a *letter opener*, after I gave him the karate chop. After I smelled the so-called vitamin serum. I wanted him to *pay* for what he did to me. Then I started thinking about how ridiculous he was, and helpless—helplessly in love with me. I just kicked him, maybe ten times, then I left him for the security people. But *you* must know about pursuit by men; you're a pretty girl too, Willis. In fact, I think we look somewhat alike."

There was a pause. Each symmetrical eye of my own looked into a separately wandering one of hers.

"We could be taken for sisters, nearly. Except perhaps for the eyes."

"The eyes."

"Yes. Mine are *so* chocolate brown and yours are green."

"Oh, yeah. Yeah, it's a significant resemblance otherwise."

"You know, Willis," she said, "it's difficult to be a beautiful woman in this world, don't you think? I mean, for me, apart from this tiny handicap, my arm here, I'm a goddess. But I don't want to complain too much about that difficulty, about the nagging thousands of would-be lovers, who I spurn because I just don't want cheap physical love. I mean, I should remind myself how lucky I am, how fortunate. To have this kind of beauty, when others are so deprived."

"Do you mind if I ask you . . . how you lost your arm?"

She closed both eyes; she looked as if she were about to "recite."

"Oh, no, of course not. It was an accident, a *freak* accident. I was a little girl, nine years old. My mother, my beautiful mother—her hair was bright red and she wore it in a French twist—had taken me to the park to get some ice cream. It was very hot, we wore thin sundresses and white shoes. I remember *everything*. I remember how *cool* Mother looked, even though it was scorching—and how she smelled: lily-of-the-valley talcum powder. We stood in line a long time at the ice cream truck—Mr. Yummy, it was. One of the ones that rolls up, opens a window, and serves the whole neighborhood. I remember the music-box chimes playing 'Beautiful Dreamer.' It was so hot in line that I started to complain, and my mother said, 'Iris, don't fret. It won't help anything, won't make it go faster if you fret, will it? Look,' she said, 'there's a little boy who's crippled and he's not complaining at all, see? Don't look right away, but see?' And I was ashamed of myself, and then it was almost our turn, we were *next*, and I was thinking about whether I wanted a double-fudge nut or a peach Dreamsicle. I reached up with my right hand, my quarter in my right hand—see?—and looked at the ice-cream man's face and . . . Then there was a noise so loud that you couldn't *hear* it. You know what I mean? It was like being hit by an invisible semi, a fifty-ton truck going ninety miles an hour, hitting you head-on. And then I was flying through the air, and then I was *on fire* flying through the air, and then I felt something hit me in the air and smash right through my teeth, then suddenly I heard screams and shouts and my arm felt like a candle, like wax burning at my shoulder. But I kept thinking: *Dreamsicle, Dreamsicle.* My hair was burning, I smelled it, and I remember thinking how will I find my mother with my arm gone? And then I hit something very hard—and I was knocked out.

"Well, there'd been an explosion. The ice-cream truck blew up. It blew up because it had a gas-powered generator that had a leak that ran down the gas line from the carburetor and dripped on the muffler and caught fire and blew up the truck's gas tank. Four people were killed: my mother, the ice-cream man, a little girl, and the crippled boy. I *think* the crippled boy, but it may not be true. I woke up in the hospital—in a plastic tent, with a strange clear tube full of green liquid where my arm had been. Or maybe there was none. Just air. When I got a little better, the plastic surgeons started. Willis, they're geniuses. I mean, they worked on me night and day, and look at this *miracle*—they saved my beauty and actually made me *more* beautiful than I was before. Though not as beautiful as my poor dead mother—red hair, chocolate-brown eyes. . . ."

She fished out a pocket mirror and fluffed out the Afro wig, licked her jagged lips, making a kissy-face, smoothing on a little lip gloss. One eye winked at me.

Then she smiled at me, straight at me; her pinwheel eyes stopped turning. A ray of sun caught her full-face; like the moon she sent the ray back to earth: the scars shone, her eyes held me in an expression so sweet I could see all of it; she was *right*. In that moment she *was* beautiful. Iris Moss was the loveliest woman in the world.

Later that day, on my way to lunch with Page, I thought about her last remark. She'd jumped up suddenly, her hand over one ear.

"Wait," she said. "Wait—God's talking to me now."

She nodded and smiled a few times. "Okay, okay, right. *Wait* on killing the president? That's a joke," she said aside to me. "But listen." The fingers grabbed me again. "This one's for *you*. . . . God says letters are a good way to 'read' people, to get to know them. Everybody on this earth should have a Letter of Identification to carry around to explain who one is. God knows about the Letters, Digby. The advice is: Don't let letters keep life away from you. Letters should bring life up close."

Six

When I told Terence I was pregnant it was in an Upper East Side apartment that belonged to two famous midgets. Well, okay, not midgets exactly, but let's say individuals of limited size. *She* was a googly-eyed comedienne whose fame dated from live TV variety show days, and *he* was the tiny producer of very big budget films. Terence was subletting their apartment from Thanksgiving through Valentine's Day, roughly the run, on Broadway, of his role in *Tiresias* (he called it first and second lead)—a pastiche of the blind hermaphrodite's wittiest sayings and favorite songs. He was Tiresias Number Four in the long and successful run.

The apartment was spacious but cluttered, and I never got used to the furniture. The famous midgets had scaled all their Louis Quinze down to a height more comfortable for them, which meant that when persons of normal size sat down, they appeared to be relieving themselves on the Aubusson.

The day I found out I was pregnant was December seventeenth, my birthday, right before Christmas, and I was giving a SIS talk at the University of Pennsylvania. I had spent the entire day driving there with Page (the result of our not grasping clearly the little mileage scale at the bottom margin of the Triple A map).

My talk was "Women's Liberation—the Next Ten Years," and I'd been so lethargic the weeks preceding I hadn't prepared much of anything to say—I'd ended up ripping a few pages of quotes from the Book of Holly Partz.

Just before the talk was to begin, I called my gynecologist in New York City.

"It was positive," the nurse-secretary said. She sounded tired.

"Positive," I repeated stupidly. "You mean I'm pregnant?"

"Yes," she said wearily, "that's how it works, Toots."

I put down the phone, walked out of the office my host had lent me as a "private place to look over my notes," and drifted down the hall and into the library lecture room. There was a podium, a microphone—fifty or so expectant faces.

Someone introduced me; I got up and stood in front of the microphone and listened to myself breathing—I'd just realized that I was drawing breath now for someone besides myself. I smiled. The audience grinned back nervously. I must have looked strange, standing there listing a little, breathing audibly the sweet, pregnant air of the University of Pennsylvania.

"I'm positive," I said into the mike. The audience looked at me. "I'm positive," I repeated, then added, floundering, "that I wore a diaphragm." Someone tittered.

I snapped awake. "This is a quote clinicians hear regularly from women and underscores why solving our birth control dilemma, the inadequacy of contraception available, is the central issue facing us as we look ahead to the next ten years of the movement."

I noticed Page shaking her head in relief. We drove home after an endless dinner party, through a snowstorm in the mountains. I never left the wheel. I looked over at Page, fast asleep, curled into her leather jacket, her head bouncing against the passenger door, feet against the heater. I felt tenderness for her, sleeping away, unaware of the enormous change sitting next to her. Through the long hours of blowing white, parted briefly, regularly, by the windshield wipers, my eyes hurt, my neck hurt—but I hunched forward feeling wonderful: I was carrying a child.

Did it matter whose child? Oh, yes, yes. I had never wanted a kid before—but suddenly I was with somebody I could imagine as a father (perhaps because he was already a father). I could imagine us, mid-thirty-type grown-up parents who loved each other and loved our kid.

We had lived together for three years. I *knew* Terence—I couldn't wait to see his face when I told him.

As I drove through the Upper West Side at 4 A.M., taking Page home, I saw his face as clearly as if it were before me, perfectly radiant. He touched me. He said, "Willy, God, Willy: our baby!"

"I'm pregnant," I whispered in his ear. He was in bed, rolled around a couple of pillows—in the king-sized bed of the midgets (how did they clamber up its daunting height, and did they swing their tiny feet over the edge?). He reached over and patted my stomach gently, he murmured something, but was asleep again in a second, so I knew he hadn't really heard.

I lay there and thought about it being an "accident." "There are no accidents," my friend Page says, I suspect because Werner Earache or some other self-actualization schmuck told her that, but she was right this time. I had wanted this baby to happen—it had only taken its becoming real to convince me.

The next day Terence was gone early—it was Saturday: two shows, matinee and evening—and rehearsal time before the first. I heard him gargling and running through a few troublesome lines in the bathroom about nine in the morning. "Desire, Zeus, desire!" I heard him intone. "Desire links god and mortal," he croaked, and gargled and flushed the toilet. I hope I'm not making him sound like an asshole. Because he was not the kind of asshole some actors are: He did not wear leather pants or go to tanning salons or speak in a fake basso profundo at the deli. He did not interrupt normal human discourse constantly with references to "points," "TVQ," and "the sweeps." He did not use coke, or hadn't for a long time, like everyone else, and if he did anything at all actorly, it was an occasional overembellishment of a description, a memory of truffles sliced on penne in Perugia or something. "Rubber baby buggy bumpers! Rubber baby buggy bumpers!" I heard him declaim, an old warm-up exercise for the thespian tongue—but it seemed sweetly apt this morning. What I'm trying to say is that Terence's sense of himself as an actor was so innate that he didn't seem like an actor—but it was always there, a concentration that never ceased. It made him seem strong.

This frame of mind also kept him suggestible—passionate convictions stuck to his consciousness like static cling to a polyester skirt.

When I met him, interviewing him for a special supplement SIS ran one fall called "Feminist Men," I couldn't believe my ears. He said things like "Women should run the country, men should not be allowed to vote until they've spent a year running a household or working as midwives." I sat on the edge of my chair in his small dressing room in the theater on Broadway and 52nd and looked at him in the mirror, taking off the makeup of Pancho Villa and talking about child care centers, and I fell in love. "Never trust a guy who says he's a feminist," was Page's comment when I floated back to SIS to type up his remarks. But I didn't listen.

I slept until late afternoon. He called around five, he was just out for a light supper at Joe Allen's before the eight o'clock curtain—no time to talk. He didn't mention anything about the night before. I contemplated getting dressed and taxiing over to the theater, but it was sleeting and I'd already seen the play about fifteen times. I decided to build a fire, put some bubbly on chill, wait for him. (We'd planned to celebrate my birthday the following night, Sunday, which he had off.)

"What a gift," I thought, hugging myself, taking a peek at my still-flat stomach. "What a gift."

"Wow," said Terence. "Unbelievable, Will." He leaned against the kitchen doorjamb, a glass of champagne in his hand. He looked tired, his curly hair rumpled, dark circles under his matinee idol's eyes. It was 12:30 A.M.

"We've been using something, haven't we?"

"I thought so," I said, "but I've been thinking back. You know, we've been slipping up a lot lately, overlooking things. . . ." I laughed conspiratorially, chinked his glass with mine. "Subconsciously, we must have meant it to happen!"

He looked at me. "Will. We didn't mean this to happen."

A little frost in the air. I smiled. He started talking about "problems." I stopped listening. I didn't want to start feeling bad. I just felt too good.

He walked into the living room. He sat down hard on a teeny chair and cursed as the champagne sloshed on his shirt. He set the glass on the weenie-roast-height table and dabbed halfheartedly at the spreading stain. Then he put his head in his hands.

This was not the radiant papa I'd pictured. I followed him into the living room and adjusted my fall into the squat chair opposite him. The firelight enlarged our reflections in the black glass: giants in a child's playhouse.

"Are you serious about this?" he asked. "You want to have this . . . kid?"

I felt great again. He was going to raise all the routine objections, and I was going to shoot them down. I'd already practiced this argument in my head—with myself—trying to figure out why the hell I did want this kid. I talked about the difficulties of our lives: his traveling, my demanding job, our mutual desire for freedom and independence. I was rational but passionate. I was witty and self-deprecating. I told jokes.

The straw opponents tumbled one by one. I could do it. *We* could do it. I stopped myself just short of promising him more freedom than I would have—I stopped myself before offering to handle diaper duty full-time, to take the late-night feedings on my own. Me, a feminist, close to that brink!

I was on that brink.

I took his hand. "Hey," I said, "we love each other."

He pulled his hand away. He drank down his champagne, got up with some difficulty and crossed the room to the bank of windows that looked out over the East River. It had started to snow: the same storm that had chased me across Pennsylvania. It bore down on Manhattan's towers and stone gargoyles, it guttered the lights on the bridge.

"I've been through this before, you know. I *can't* go through it again."

When Terence was nineteen, he'd knocked up a South African girl. Her unsuccessful but enterprising father (mastermind of several failed import schemes), in a final attempt to balance his personal trade deficit, had taken his family of five eager daughters traveling through the United States. Pressure was brought to bear on Terence. He and Candy were married and had Troy. Their alliance went, predictably, down the drain, but it lasted long enough to force Terence to drop out of college and out of the acting conservatory. Then came the squeeze. The Ex had been living cheekily in Johannesburg on Terence's alimony (along with her new boyfriend and two new kids) ever since the divorce. She'd kept Troy for a while, then sent him winging to Terence, who paid for expensive boarding schools. Terence also paid for Troy's occasional holiday visits to fun-filled Afrikaner-land—this Christmas, for example. Terence's role in all this was to feel guilty a lot and Ex's was to take her alimony checks and contribute absolutely zip to Troy's upbringing but the occasional poison-pen letter disguised as friendly chat, telling Terence what a rotten father he was.

"That," I said, "was different."

He turned around to look at me. "Why?"

I didn't answer. I got up very slowly. I put the tulip glass down on a wee table. I felt nauseated. Could it be morning sickness already? Over in the corner stood a squat Christmas tree that I'd hauled in and hung with liquidy gold ornaments. Beneath its stunted boughs were stacked the gold-wrapped presents for Terence. The brightness hurt my eyes.

I stood beside him at the window, watching the whole universe come apart, shake loose into a billion crystals.

"Because," I said, "you know that line in *Tiresias* when the gods ask him about sexual pleasure and he says that a woman's orgasmic experience outdoes a man's ten thousand by ten thousand?"

"Yeah?" He looked cockily, expectantly at me.

"Well," I said, "my experience with you has never been like *that*. What I feel with you is what a homing pigeon must feel, rowing through the air, way up, some metal on its leg: I just have to make it home to you."

He turned away. I heard him behind me fiddling with the champagne, pulling the bottle out of the ice and pouring himself another glass.

Carol Muske-Dukes

When he stood next to me again, he seemed almost cheerful. He put his arm around me; he kissed my neck.

"You *know* what you got to do, Will."

I watched the lights of the bridge stuttering on and off in the snow. Now don't get me wrong. I'm no stranger to abortion. And I worked at SIS, for God's sake, I supported the politics of choice. But somehow this was different. "Why?" he'd asked, and finally I just couldn't say. Somebody wanted to be born, I wanted to say. But that was a little too Yeatsian. His false cheer only made me more determined.

"I love you," he added, an afterthought. I thought of the skewed etiquette of the late twentieth century. All those "supportive" boyfriends and husbands and lovers standing around lamely in the track-lit lounges of the posh little outpatient clinics around Manhattan, reading the Op Ed page two hundred times. Trying not to sound possessive, just the right note of concern: "How's she doing, nurse?"

But it wasn't that either. *This is Lily*, I thought suddenly. Lily. My daughter.

He began to talk very animatedly about his career, and I tried to listen with sympathy. Yes, he'd finally reached the point he'd longed for, he was getting *close* . . . he was getting Broadway and film and television offers. Some leading-man parts. All his life he'd fought for this. He was convincing; my heart did go out to him. I could see him at twenty, a backstage carpenter, the young struggling thespian. The guy who comes and goes in *Henry IV* or *Richard II* and announces things: gardener, keep, messenger, groom.

Servant: "My Lord, your son was gone before I came."

What did he want with another kid? A set builder, supporting a family when other guys were spilling beer on each other at frat parties. I could see that imprisoned, frustrated youth. The thing was, he was also the person standing in front of me, my lover, fifteen years later, a successful actor. And all those nights I'd reached for the diaphragm and he'd pulled my hand back.

"Listen, Terence," I interrupted. "I love you too. I'm not going to be a millstone around your neck. I'm sorry about your former life and your shitty ex-wife. I'm not going to be a millstone around your neck, but I'm going to have this kid. On my own, if I have to."

I went into the bedroom and sat on the king-sized bed. Snow drifted down outside the French doors. It covered the terrace and blew up the downspouts with a single clear note like Peruvian pipes.

I had to scrunch to see myself in the vanity mirror. "Hi, little mother," I growled. Then, *sotto voce,* in a voice I tried to make sound male, paternal: "What great news, honey. I'd hoped this would happen. Happy *birth*day!" I touched my stomach. "Happy birthday to you, Lily." Then I pulled off my clothes, pulled on a nightgown, and went to bed.

The next day I wandered into St. Pat's. I lit a candle, I stopped at each of the Stations of the Cross, a pastime whose peculiar appeal only ex-Catholics can appreciate. Veronica Wiping the Face of Jesus was always my favorite. I thought of her as the first Fan Club president. I sat in a pew and looked at the altar, still covered in Advent purple. Could I be a single parent? Dear God, I prayed, give me a miracle, I need a miracle now.

When I went outside, it was warming up, the snow was melting. I walked along Fifth Avenue, then over to Park. I looked at a few fat babies in their strollers. Could I raise a kid alone?

I bought a container of rice pudding and a souvlaki: I'd been craving both. I nodded to the doorman and took the elevator to the top floor. Terence was just unlocking the apartment door—he spun around when the elevator opened.

He looked unearthly. He wore a flight jacket and jeans, but he'd dressed in such a hurry he'd left his last-act *Tiresias* makeup on—in the final scene he was half and half, split right down the middle. There was a heavy pancake tan, a dark beard and mustache and shaggy brow on one side of his face. The other side was clean-shaven, pale, with half a Cupid's-bow mouth below one false eyelash and a perfectly made-up woman's eye. He wore one dangling diamond earring and one sideburn.

Both sexes looked pretty depressed. "Willie," he gasped. "*All right*. Let's get married. Let's just do it and get it over with!"

A neighbor came out of the apartment next door and looked, looked again, then hurried off, stealing backward glances all the way. Terence whirled around and glared after him. The earring shook.

"Would you mind turning your head?" I asked. "I think I'd rather be proposed to by a man."

The made-up eye winked. "Sure."

"I can't promise how long I'll stay," the beard said. "This is very hard on me, you know. The commitment."

"Okay. That's enough. I changed my mind, could you turn the other way again? I think I prefer the woman."

Page was my best woman at City Hall. She took this opportunity to confer a great deal of unsolicited advice on the bride. She waited till we were both a little sloshed at the reception for thirty or so that Terence and I threw at a posh hotel on the water.

She was eating caviar on tiny toasts, and crumbs showered into her satin bodice. She fished them out cheerfully, crossing her eyes, as she searched her cleavage. She lifted her champagne glass. "The only time a woman who marries an actor gets top billing is on her gravestone." She pulled at the sleeve of my off-off-off white dress, snorting a little, spilling "Cristal." She clutched my arm. "But don't go *that* far to get it!"

Page had been married at twenty-one to an aspiring soap opera star of twenty-six. They divorced when she was twenty-three, but he claimed he was only twenty-two in the divorce papers. "At that rate," she said, "if we'd waited till our silver anniversary to divorce, he'd have been a fertilized egg." (Her ex, Garth Narrows, was now featured on the daytime drama "Escape from Nuance.")

I kept my old apartment down in Gramercy Park, and we hung out at the Midget Palace while looking for new digs. The midgets extended the lease. *I* looked for new digs. Terence was performing a lot and couldn't find the time, so I ended up looking alone. "Be careful," my doctor warned. She tapped my swollen abdomen gently with her stethoscope. "The first months are touchy."

Terence stopped wanting to make love. "What's the matter?" I asked. We were in the wee people's king-sized bed and it was raining outside. There were satin sheets and there was a candle going. We'd always had a great sex life. "What's the matter?" I asked again forlornly. My breasts were blooming and my middle had that first sweet curving swell. Yes, I'd studied it—I'd been thinking I looked quite fetching that very night after dropping my bath towel in front of the full-length mirror. I looked over at him. He hadn't told me once that he liked the way I looked. It had occurred to me to ask him to *act* a little, feign a little interest. He sighed and rolled over. I stared at his back.

At three months I felt established as a pregnant person; I went into work every day and answered the endless letters with real officiousness. I ate green leafy vegetables and listened to Minnie W-W-G's lectures on Baby Names. It was hard work, looking for apartments—I climbed stairs, puff-ing—everything I saw seemed wrong.

One afternoon I had to lie down. I was exhausted, a funny wired kind of exhaustion. I felt knocked out, but revved up in some way. I got up to go to the john and saw the first blood.

"Nothing to worry about," the doctor reassured me on the phone. Her name was Dr. Denny Bright. "This happens all the time at the end of the first trimester," she said, "but if you want me to check you I will."

By the time I got to her office, the blood was serious, and by the time Terence got out of the last show at eleven, I was in the hospital. I had miscarried and I was slightly sedated. But not enough.

"Please get the fuck out of here," I said clearly, calmly, when I saw him and I could speak.

For weeks after that, we lay next to each other in the midgets' big bed, not touching. After a while I drifted back downtown to my old apartment. Terence was offered a mini-series that shot in Liverpool and Luxor called *So What, Sun Ra?*, or something like that. His role was a narc, a really fine part—he got to wear a trenchcoat and have a tic.

We said good-bye on the phone. Our conversation didn't last long. It turned out that there really wasn't much else to say.

Seven

Dear Letters Editor,

You send me that smart-ass answer in the mail, then I seen here you printed my letter in your column and dragged my butt over the coals in public. You gotta lot of nerves, Digby. When I say I don like something IT MEANS WATCH OUT BELOW. I'M SAYIN IT NOW—THIS I DON'T LIKE. Your in for it now sister.

Sincerely,
Dino Pedrelli

Dear Willis,

Keep up the good work! I think you are great! Here's a pair of socks I knitted for you (one size fits all!) sorry about the dropt stitches! Could you take a photo of your feet wearing them and send to me by return mail?

Yours,
Lulu Lagerfelt

P.S. Glad you told those pigs off!

I noticed I had some mail from The Watcher, another faithful correspondent. The Watcher sent me vaguely threatening notes, which were also vaguely poetic. The first one I'd gotten months earlier, right after Terence had gone off to his miniseries.

Dear Willis Digby,

Although the lamp is out, I can see fairly clearly in the reflected light from other buildings: pigeons, scaffolding, a window washer's pail and sponge touched by a ray. Then suddenly it's darker—and I can see you. I pull the telescope over. You're working late tonight, like me. Working late, your head bowed over a pile of papers. Every once in a while you look up, murmur something to yourself, then sink back into a little chasm of shadow. You're lovely, Willis, I can see it clearly—even when you pull your hair severely back and wear strange things on your head. Even when you wear men's clothing. You were wearing clothes like that the morning I first saw you. I passed by your building and you were on the street talking to the mailman, who was standing there with all those overflowing mail sacks for SIS. You were laughing; you said: "I'm Willis Digby, what kind of bribe would it take to get you to stop bringing this stuff?"

You have a bright face, meant to be happy. But something has hurt you. I can tell as I watch you. Sometimes you stare at the wall, you twirl your hair, you look inexpressibly sad. I wish I knew what has hurt you. Maybe I do. Maybe you need to talk to someone like me. Someone who watches over you.

The Watcher

I looked out the SIS windows at the surrounding buildings—nothing but office towers. One to one hundred floors.
Attorneys, magazines, public relations, holding companies.
He could be in any one of them. I felt so vulnerable, so "un-
taken care of" I almost began to enjoy knowing he was out
there. A mad guardian angel. He wrote a lot. Same type of
letter.

I met a famous "Advice to the Lovelorn" columnist. She
was seated next to me at a luncheon for women journalists,
and I immediately began picking her brains about letters.
She was plucky and staunch, a small, pretty, no-nonsense
woman in her late fifties, with the immobile mandible of the
face-lifted. She said she got a thousand letters a day (her
column appeared daily in newspapers all over the country),
which put things more in perspective for me, though the
solace didn't last long. She also said that crazy letters were
obvious and that she disregarded them. She said you could
always tell the real psychos by the handwriting. She said
that it was usually large, sloping, half off the page, or small,
frenzied, and misshapen. The Watcher certainly fit the bill
here—his tiny fevered script with all its blots and crossings-
out looked like an exploded ant farm. "In all these years I've
never had any personal dealings with any of my correspondents, honey" then added, her voice dropping, "it's *never* a
good idea."

The Watcher had a whole lot to say to me about me. He
knew nothing about me, I decided, but his speculations were
often startlingly perceptive. At the worst of my "what a lousy
year it's been" depression, he wrote an oddly insightful letter
about children. Did my sadness have anything to do with
children? Or childhood? He could see that I looked down,
he could see I needed someone to talk to. There was "a child
dying" in my face, he said. I showed this letter to Page, who
said, "Willis, look at me. Is there a cat dying in my face?"

I was tempted to answer him, to detail my sorrows in a

letter to a total stranger (and voyeur at that!), but I resisted the impulse, I wasn't that crazy. Still, I caught myself throwing my hair back a little self-consciously when I walked through the columns of sunlight that poured through the great naked SIS windows. It was like appearing in a film— was it possible that I tried to imagine sometimes what the camera was seeing, what the camera wanted to see? Think about it. When was the last time someone watched your every move with tireless, loving eyes? You were a child, and the tender, concerned gaze belonged to the watchful totemic beings you learned to call mother and father. You know, the ones who eventually got distracted and looked away?

Dear Digby,

I saw you at Padgett's Deli. You have the most wonderful way of looking involved when you're actually daydreaming. A quotation mark of concentration appears between your brows, and you chew (very delicately) on one side of your lip. When it was your turn to order, the guy behind the counter had to say, "Miss? Miss?" three times before you came to. But you covered it beautifully. "It's the cole slaw," you said in a clear tone. "It looks particularly *fine* today."

Dear Digby,

This afternoon you were in the lobby of the SIS building waiting for the elevator. Nobody was around, the elevator was taking forever. Then a black guy with a ghetto blaster took up position in the lobby doorway— he was parked like a sound truck, 200 decibels of "Heartbreak Hotel." You looked guilty for a split second, checked to be sure you were alone, then launched into a really funky Elvis imitation for the lobby mirrors. You rolled your hips, twisted down to the floor, held an invisible mike to your sneering lips. You stomped and wailed and wept and shook your hair, and when the elevator arrived (with that curmudgeonly elevator operator), you stopped cold, instantly. You adjusted your collar haughtily before boarding the lift. I heard you say, "What took you so long?" out of the corner of your mouth.

WJD,
   You were wearing a brilliant yellow silk scarf this morning. It was so bright it reminded me of the yellow cotton dress that a Salinger character named Charlotte wore, the dress that left a stain on Seymour's hand. Do you know the one?

Of course I did. I knew the yellow mark on Seymour's hand and his famous remark about it. How he described himself as a person who was paranoid in reverse: He suspected other people of plotting to make him happy. That happened to be one of my favorite passages in literature. It seemed the Watcher and I had somehow evolved similar literary taste, or at least he liked some of the same Great Moments, in *Richard II* and Issa and Emily Dickinson. He was eerily close to seeing through me, into my Bide-a-Wee heart.
   So why couldn't I see *him*? Which lurker-in-the-shadows *was* he? The guy in the knit cap and sunglasses in the deli? The pale, apologetic gent in the three-piece suit at the bus stop? A cabbie? A cook? Who? I focused on certain faces— would he have a mustache like that? An overbite? A Stones T-shirt or Mojo root? Dredlocks? I became self-conscious in the subway, in the coffee line.
   He called himself an "artist-seer."

"Artist-*schmartist*. The guy's a voyeur," Page wailed, outraged, sifting through his missives. "Bear this in mind, Willis. He's no better than your average Peeping Tom, he just talks posh."

Dear Digby,
    I've given you my P.O. Box Number, my Heart File.
Why don't you write to me? Please, please, write to me.

I'd sent out a few unconventional responses to letters in my time, but I couldn't bring myself to connect here. I did not write back. Still, I looked for his letters. They got more intense, even critical.

When I broke precedent and answered weird correspondents in the column, he was miffed. I spent my time coming up with smart comments for others, but not a crumb for him? Also, I'd lost an "innocent quality." One day he looked at me in late afternoon sun and my profile struck him as "sharp, desperate, predatory." (This gave rise to Page's coining of the expression, "Digby's SDP Profile." The SDP Profile had nothing to do with my emotions, she said, but rather an overdeveloped chin. Can I help it, I asked her, if I have my father's Four-Star jaw?)

Today his letter looked sealed in haste, angry. The handwriting was even more constipated than usual.

Dear Digby,
    Ah, the "folly of being comforted" (as the poet says) by what appears before the eyes. I had thought you were kind. That day I saw you, in the sunlight, laughing with the mailman, I thought I'd seen a dreamer—I loved the touching hesitancy in your manner. You seemed

hopeful, ingenuous. Now I see you are—what? A frightening mixture of fear and cynicism. I know about the actor. I read a scandal sheet the other day that linked your name with his. Is *that* the tragedy one sees in your eyes? The loss of a media huckster? How could you? I know some other things about you too. I know now, for instance, that you live at 871 East 17th Street, Apartment 7W. I know you leave for work every day around 9:15 A.M., and I see your lights go out at night. You stay up late, Digby, you must have trouble sleeping. I see you reading, then I see you throw the book down, pace, talk to yourself. Something is driving you crazy. Isn't something bothering you, something from the past? Sometimes you hold yourself and cry, you really sob. Your bedroom faces east—you get the first light. Sometimes you're still up then. The sun comes up and you look out the window at the red sky and you watch the sun come up. I watch your face turn gold, like a carved image on a sarcophagus—you look dead. You're dead inside, aren't you, Willis Digby?

I stopped reading. I threw The Watcher's letter down and stalked over to the coffee maker. I fixed myself a large white coffee with the horrible fake cream powder and sat down again. Then I got up and held the letter in front of Page's face. "Read this."

She read it, then set it aside as if it were soaked in cat pee. "You should have called the police right away about this guy—didn't I tell you that when he first wrote to you about peering at you through the windows? Now he's on your doorstep."

She looked up at me. "You look terrible. Are you okay, Willis?"

I was *not* okay. But I sighed back to my desk and set the

letter aside for the moment and plucked another envelope from the pile.

Dear Willis,

You haven't been publishing our suggestions. No fair. We gave you our support when you needed it. You need your consciousness raised. Come out with us on a "run"—or are you too chicken? Meet us Wednesday night at seven, at Cleopatra's Needle. Don't forget to RSVP. (And don't forget to wear running shoes!)

Your friends at W.I.T.C.H

I turned the envelope and looked at the W.I.T.C.H. symbol stamped at the back.

Page had a lunch date. After she'd gone, I picked up the phone. I called the *Daily Mirror* and asked for the city desk. I told the guy who answered about Iris Moss and the hypno-rapist of Brookheart. He asked a lot of questions. I heard computer blips in the background.

"An *orderly*," I said. "Isn't that interesting? What is an orderly doing giving out medication in the first place?"

"Who can confirm all this?" the editor asked.

I gave Iris's name. "She resides at Brookheart."

The guy laughed. "*C'mon*, Ms. Digby. You mean to say she's one of the crazy people? *She* gave you the story?"

"Now who would be in a better position to know about patient abuse than a patient?"

After I hung up, I sat for a while, staring at the pile of letters. I looked over at my rabbit ears. They'd grown dusty in recent days. I blew the dust off. I looked at them fondly for a while. I put them on.

Dear Dino,

Wise up. You write a letter to the editor at a magazine or newspaper, you relinquish your rights to it. You were *lucky* enough to get published in SIS. Look at it that way, scrotum-head.

Yrs,
WJD

Dear W.I.T.C.H.,

Okay, I'd like to go on a "run" with you. I will be there at Cleopatra's Needle in the Park, Wednesday night at seven. I'll be the one wearing rabbit ears.

In struggle,
Sister Digby

Then I pulled out the threatening letter. It was signed, as usual, The Watcher. I edited the letter, taking out the more blatant personal references—my address, etc.—leaving basically the fact of the threat: that this guy had my home address and was spying on me.

My hands were shaking. On yellow copy paper I roughed out an answer.

Dear Watcher,

I want my readers to know that you've written to me before. Many times, in fact. Always your letters have referred to the fact that you are watching me. Watching me from the office building where you work, through your telescope. Watching me on the street, at the lunch counter, the pharmacy, when I have no idea I'm being observed. How many times have you asked me to write back to you at your post office box, to be your friend?

Well, here I am. I'm writing back now, publicly, because I would like other women to witness *you*, to witness the kind of cheap, threatening bully you really are. Men who make obscene phone calls. Men who write anonymous threats to women, men who follow women on the street—you're all the same. I will not be your friend. Nor will I be afraid of you. I'm going to call the police, and I'm also going to give you fair warning. If you keep on violating my right to privacy, don't count on me to be a scared, defenseless victim. If you try to threaten me physically in any way: the victim, pal, I promise you, will be you.

Sincerely,
Willis J. Digby
Letters Editor

I put my answer to the W.I.T.C.H. letter in the regular mail slot and put the note to Dino and the one to The Watcher in the big red DEADLINE COPY basket. All copy for the magazine was supposed to be approved by the SIS collective editorial board—but my letters often slipped by without group review. Over the years trust had developed for my odd selection process and for the fact that I was a maverick. Too much trouble to argue with.

I threw another couple of letters (one from my favorite U.F.O. spotter), with instructions to the printer, in the same deadline basket. I'd made Xerox copies of everything. I shoved these in my bag and went out whistling. As I rounded the corner of 43rd and Lex, I felt a very purposeful tap on my shoulder, and I nearly lost consciousness.

It was Terence.

I took an involuntary step toward him, in relief, then pulled back.

"When did *you* get back?"

He was looking at me strangely. "About a month ago."

I looked away. "A *month*?"

"Willis?" His face was concerned. "Why are you wearing those rabbit ears?"

We went to a little café on Lex and sat across from each other at a tiny wobbly table. "Shades of the midgets," I joked, but he only looked sad.

The waiter brought wine, and I drank some quickly. I was feeling, even with the rabbit ears safely tucked away in my bag, not exactly normal. I forced myself to look at him. He looked away, which gave me a chance to see that he was starring, as always, in his own show: trim, tan, clean-shaven.

"You look great."

He smiled and looked at me finally. "So do you. Except for the rabbit ears."

"When I get the weirdest letters, they act as an antenna. They help sort out transmissions for me . . . ha ha."

He frowned.

I sat forward. I needed to talk to somebody.

"I've been getting some very *strange* letters lately."

He snorted. "So what else is new at SIS's Crackpot Desk?"

"But listen to this: I've started answering the letters!"

He raised an eyebrow, sipped and listened to my story. How I'd let a tidal wave of this stuff pound over me, how one day I picked up a pen and wrote back, got SIS to agree to publish the odd letters and my even odder responses. Even as I spoke I had a sense of aspects of the story whirring and clicking into place, overpolished, apochryphal. I lifted my glass, inviting a toast.

"I'm on my way to becoming the liberated woman's Dear Abby—okay, no, it's sleazier. I'm like a late night talk show host, a Joe Pine, who insults people who call in."

Terence touched my glass but looked skeptical.

"It's a *great* idea" I said. "It makes me feel one hundred percent better. It's just that I have to be . . . careful."

"Damn right. You start writing back to some of those bananas and . . ."

Just then a fan came up—a determined woman from Queens who had seen him in *Large Dead Cops*, or something like that; I didn't catch it all. I had grown used to this kind of interruption. It was profoundly humbling, really, being with someone famous, or someone somewhat famous. I kept forgetting that Terence was a figure in the imaginings of other people. Once at dinner in an intimate restaurant, a menu, wielded like a placard, sliced between our heads (bent passionately close over the low candle) and a voice that sounded like Selma Diamond yodeling on speed split the air around us. The woman plunked herself down at our table.

"Sign right here," she commanded Terence. I stared, struggling to understand why this was happening. She looked back at me and winked. "Gotta quarter?"

Now I sat and smiled benignly as Terence signed and wrote special greetings to grandchildren and bowling partners. I drank some more wine.

I thought back to the first time Terence and I went out to a "public" do, an opening night of some sort. We got out of the car holding hands, and a young man with a camera asked for a shot of Terence "alone." I smiled over at Terence as if to say, "What brass!" Terence gave me a gimlet eye, then a quick nod that meant "move it, Myrtle."

I, Myrtle, moved it. Now I could see him kindly trying to hurry the woman along—turning down (astonishingly) an invitation to appear at her bowling league banquet.

Still, our mood was kind of lost.

I ordered some more wine. "I suppose you're aware that we're still husband and wife?" I asked, with the terrible coyness a second glass always lends.

"What do we do about it?" He looked grief-stricken suddenly. He cupped one hand over his left eye, squinting at me as if I were a high-intensity bulb. He sighed, collapsing into himself: a beaten man. It was diverting, but I remained unmoved. I recognized these gestures from a film he wished he'd never made (and I wished I'd never seen) called *Condo Bondage*, or something like that. He had terrible unconscious throwbacks (in moments of stress) to the physical movements of his character in that flick. Something like LSD flashbacks.

I pushed ahead.

"We divorce, right?"

He shrugged. "Right, I guess."

I was getting depressed. "You wanna sue me or should I sue you?"

Carol Muske-Dukes

"On what grounds?"

"I could sue you for mental cruelty," I said helpfully, trying to grease the wheels.

"Mental cruelty? . . . Mental cruelty? That's interesting. I was actually thinking that I might sue *you* for mental cruelty."

"That *is* interesting. Well, I could go with . . . what's that archaic-sounding charge? 'Refusal to cohabit' or something like that? I was leaning in that direction too. You know the one, when one of the partners refuses to . . ."

"Yeah," he said quickly. "I know. So what you're saying is that there was physical incompatibility."

"And spiritual."

"Ah!" He finished his wine with a flourish. "Ah! Spiritual as well! Then I suppose that accounts for the rather large debit on your side of the ledger; I guess we could call it willful abandonment of your spouse."

"Abandonment!" I whooped. The couple next to us looked over. "That's rich! I abandoned *you*? You abandoned me every time we entered a room with a mirror."

"Who left our *domicile*, huh? With forethought and malice? Who moved out on me? Back into her place downtown that she never gave up?"

"Who went to goddamn Egypt?" I squawked. The couple was staring unabashedly. "Did I go to Egypt? Did I see the pyramids? Nooooo, *you* were the one who got to boogey with Tut!"

Terence turned and smiled at the couple. They smiled back with a dreamy tenderness at him, gradually recognizing him from something—a TV drama, a play.

"Give 'em the teeth, Terence," I said, hating myself.

He got up. I got up. He threw money on the table. I threw money on the table. Then I reconsidered and took back a dollar or two.

"Listen," I said, "in New York all you have to do is file

for separation and stay separated for a year and divorce is automatic: no fault."

He turned up his jacket collar, put on his sunglasses, and growled, "No fault, my ass." Then he looked at the floor. "Fine, let's get it over with."

"That's what you said on our wedding day, do you remember?"

He shook his head sadly.

"I'll file for separation," I said.

We marched out. Bright sun. We said a terse good-bye on the curb—what else was there to say?

Nine

I opened the New York *Mirror* and there it was—*Exclusive to the Mirror*—reports of sexual abuse of patients by staff at Brookheart State Hospital. It headlined low on the front page, but it was a long, well-researched article that meandered back through the first section.

Patient charges of sexual abuse were substantiated by secret staff sources, a part-time physician, *and* a reporter posing as a nurse.

One patient, quoted extensively throughout the article, maintained that the abuse had been going on for five years or longer. Another patient pointed out specifics of the violation:

> I am aware of my physical attractiveness but I am no bimbo! When I first understood that I was being abused (I was drugged and seminal fluid was being pumped into my precious body against my will), I became so angry that I vowed that I would kill my tormentors if I ever lay eyes on them.

It's bad enough being crazy, without having to contend with seminal fluid.

The article went on to describe items recovered from patients as possible evidence of wrongdoing: a syringe filled with chloral hydrate allegedly used to sedate victims, S & M paraphernalia found in a male nurse's file drawer, some photographs of Brookheart patients in pornographic poses taken from an administrator's desk drawer by a patient.

The State District Attorney's office is expected to announce an investigation of patient allegations and will begin to subpoena witnesses next week.

I put the paper down. I was working late. Outside the windows the lights were coming on at seventy stories and up. What a sight in the pink dusk! *What a world,* I thought. I laughed out loud and threw my rabbit ears up in the air. *What a world, Iris!* Then: *Way to go, Iris!*

The last mailbag of the day leered at me from the shadows. I pulled it to me like a lover. I could stand anything now—Iris was an inspiration! I shook the bag upside down, and the postmarked shower fell.

I tore one open at random.

Dear Letters Editor,

I *love* your new format! I thought your comeback to the redneck sexist creep really put him in his place! And your answer to that psychotic Peeping Tom: bravo. I'll bet no one's ever published a letter like *that* before! Keep up the good work!

A Reader

There were fifty or so enthusiastic letters in the same vein—lots of them from women who had received weird communications: letters, phone calls, street assaults. Anonymous notes under the door.

And there were some dead set *against* the new style. They were a distinct minority, but very outspoken:

Are you kidding? *Letters* was a serious information column, now it's a forum for retards!

and:

Cancel my subscription at once! "WJD" has insulted every thinking reader, woman or man, with her smart-aleck sewer-talk!

and:

Letters like that should never see the light! To publish them, not to mention *respond* to them, invites disaster, puts everyone in the dark!

A note from Iris at the bottom of one pile, dotted with smiling faces and stars:

Dear Willis,

I talked to a newspaper reporter last week who said you preferred to remain anonymous, but that you were the one who tipped them off to Basil Schrantz, etc. They're all over the place now—it's great!! I gave them all the facts and showed them my collection of seminal-fluid-stained panties from the last *two* years! Wow, were they impressed!

Please come up to Brookheart, next Thursday in the afternoon, for our Crafts Fair. I'll introduce you around;

I'll show you my room and my yucca plant and my Hot Line to the Supreme Somewhat Preoccupied Intelligence.

I took a pen and wrote on the bottom of her letter: "Will be there Thursday," and sent it off.

There was also a letter from Terence, marked PERSONAL AND CONFIDENTIAL.

Dear Letters Editor,

Since we don't seem to be able to communicate any other way, I thought I'd write to you. Let's hold off on the separation proceedings for the time being. Okay? We're both too angry to approach the problem rationally right now. Would you like to meet again for an *attempt* at conversation? Just call and tell me *when*. Call 555–2722.

Sincerely, your erstwhile husband,
Terence Major

I toyed briefly with the idea of publishing "Just call and tell me *when*," plus his name and phone number—but it seemed extreme, even for me.

Dear Terence,

The line's busy right now. Call back later.

Sincerely, your ersatz wife,
Willis J. Digby

P.S. Caught you on a rerun last night on the late late late—the one where you play Laverene and Shirley's deaf gynecologist? Looking back, do you think you peaked early?

One last hit, I decided, before I called it a night. I looked uneasily at the bank of windows, exposed to the city night, exposed to the curious malicious eye. I poked nervously around in the canvas bag.

"Do you have a friend or boyfriend who might play a joke like this on you?" the precinct detective asked me when I'd called the 17th and explained my situation to him.

"Jesus," I said, "of course not. What kind of friend should do something like this? Write threatening letters about window peeking?"

"Lots," he said. "We see it all the time."

"And what do you do about it?" I asked.

"Nothing," he said. "In those cases these disagreements among friends have a way of resolving themselves. Also, serious threats through the U.S. Mail are a matter for the FBI. If you really fear for your safety, we'll come down and talk to you."

"Thanks," I said. "I'll call *you*."

I found the letter I guess I had been expecting from the beginning.

Dear Digby,

Oh, the wind is cold today. The mica in the pavement burns with cold. The cold is filled with voices; they come in under the door and through the hole in the wall. They're all calling at once. All asking for mercy. Have you ever asked for mercy, Willis? Do you ever give mercy?

You printed my letter in your magazine. Then you

printed your response. So that anybody could read it.

It takes love to watch someone the way I've been watching you. Not the selfish love men usually have for women, but a different kind of love. I loved you as Time—if Time could love us. I was going to heal you, as Time can.

But you have hurt me now with your response. Don't you remember your Salinger—how in a *seer*, the eyes are the part of the human body that suffer the most? That when a *seer* is wounded, the cries come straight from the eyes? How could you forget?

Now I think I have to finish you. You are like a story I've been writing. Like a story, you're coming to an end. But you chose this ending and there are so many others. Say, "The woman walks free, smiling a little, out the door, into the light." Or, "The dreamer fell asleep in her lover's arms." No, there are other possibilities now, I suppose. "The woman picks up the gun, sucks on it, pulls the trigger," or, "A man takes a sharp knife and cuts a woman's breasts off, then cooks them and eats them," you see what I mean? I don't want to frighten you, but don't you see how the ending can go wrong now?

I stopped reading. The glass of the window was burning with the last comeback of sunset, then out. Late dusk, blue dark, the day a has-been.

. . . so remember, all of what happens from now on is your choice. You are responsible for the blood to come, the way I must cut things. This is the thing I fear, the thing I feel I was sent to you to do. Please don't be frightened. Please.

I pulled my rabbit ears off. Just then I heard a noise. It came from around the corner, past Page's and my partition. I'd assumed that I was alone. My brain began forming a very clear picture of The Watcher. His cutting instruments.

There were footsteps down the hall.

Holly Partz poked her head in.

"Great! Willis! You're here! God, I'm sorry I startled you, you look like a ghost! I *have* to talk to you!"

She sat down and smiled benignly upon my avalanche of mail.

"I just got a call from Moira Phillips at the *Mirror*. She says that you are the one who tipped them off about the Brookheart scandal. Her city editor spilled the beans. It's been confirmed by the . . . resident at Brookheart—Ms. Moss? The woman who sent you the original information? Moira wants to know if you would agree to tell your 'story.' They'd like to send someone over to interview you. Also they'd like to talk about your new 'Letters' format."

She grinned sheepishly at me. "I have to apologize, Willis. I had no faith at all in your vision of 'Letters.' I've been getting mail and phone calls all week from readers who think your approach is the best thing that's ever happened to SIS. A few don't like it at all, but *everyone's* got something to say about it."

"I know."

"Will you do the interview? Tomorrow? Here, at two?"

"Sure," I said. "What does it matter?"

"There's one other thing, Willis. Something I *don't* like. I think you went too far when you printed that personally threatening letter. I missed it on the page proofs. I would have asked you to pull it."

Silence.

"Has this person threatened you again?"

I covered The Watcher's letter with an envelope and laughed.

"Of course not," I said. "The whole thing was theater, like most of these letters. He disappeared when his bluff was called."

She looked hard at me. "I don't believe that, not for a second. Be careful, Willis. The SIS collective still has final editorial sayso—you can't keep operating on your own. And I don't want to start printing disclaimers. Nor do I want to see you in danger because of bad judgment."

"Thanks, boss."

She turned and smiled patiently at me.

"Please don't call me that, Willis, even in jest. We're all equal here, you know that."

After she left, I uncovered the letter.

Now that I know where you live, I'll come to your address to finish the story. The ending is coming.
Soon,
The Watcher

Ten

Home, I saluted Wally ("Whizzer") Herbst, the slow-talking, snow-haired doorman, slumped into the elevator and slumped off at seven. There was a smudged note taped to my door.

I recognized the crabbed handwriting before I read it.

Greetings!
   Your building should be protected better! That old guy downstairs misses a *lot*!
                                                    XXXXX
                                                    The Watcher

I decided to enter my domicile only briefly. I tore the note off the door, stuffed it in my pocket to show to the police, went in and took some money from a drawer. It was the night I was supposed to meet W.I.T.C.H. in the Park. I had earlier decided against going: I'd just changed my mind. I stood by the phone for a minute, then picked it up and dialed. I could see myself in a mirror on the wall. I looked like a person surprised to be looking in the mirror. I made a horrendous gargoyle face, just to bring myself back to normal.

"Seventeenth Precinct."

"Hi. I called once before, about a guy who's harassing me through the mails? Now he's come to my house."

"Hold on, please."

After repeating the same thing three times, I found myself talking to a Detective Blair. I explained about the letters, about the threats, about the note on my door.

"The FBI handles threats by mail, but now that he's come to your building, we can send an officer by tomorrow to talk to you."

"Tomorrow? What if he shows up tonight?"

"Ms. Digby, these harassment situations don't usually end up being a threat. This guy's done what he wanted to do: scare you. But if you want me to, I'll try to get somebody by there tonight."

"It's okay," I said. "I'm going out tonight and I'm sure not going to sleep *here*."

I put on my running shoes and went off to meet W.I.T.C.H. for an evening of carefree pleasures, but after consulting the Yellow Pages, I made a stop on the way.

"It's been a long time since I held one of these in my hand,"
I said to the guy behind the counter. He looked like a black
Ed Sullivan, but lacked Ed's dynamite charisma.

I put the .38 caliber Midnight Special on the counter between us. I looked hard at Ed. He was, presumably, skilled
at judging basket cases. I wanted him to think of me as sane
but scared enough to be desperate.

"I'm very frightened," I said. "There've been a couple of
muggings right in front of my building. I'm terrified to go
out at night." I leaned over the counter in my eagerness to
convince.

He nodded distractedly. He'd heard it all before.

"The thing is . . . I need the gun right away—I'm afraid
something might *happen*. . . ."

He nodded again. He'd heard this too.

"You see, I'm experienced with guns. My father was a
military man, and he trained me in the use of firearms, all
kinds." He had *not* often heard this from a woman, but he
didn't seem to care.

While I chattered on, he reached under the counter, fished out an Application for a License to Carry a Firearm. I began filling it out. *Have you ever been convicted of a felony in the State of New York?* Then I did something that astonished me, if not him.

I pulled a couple of very large bills from my wallet. I put them on the counter.

"I need the gun *right away*."

The guy looked at me, then at the money. He covered the bills with a *Time* magazine.

"Lemme see yer driver's license and yer other I.D."

He looked at my license, my SIS photo I.D., my credit cards, and a bank card. He looked at me again.

"Fill out the form," he snarled.

My hand shook so badly I could hardly write. What if Ed called the police? Here I was, guilty of attempted bribery. I concentrated on finishing the form. Then, as I started to tell him to forget the whole thing, I'd been joking, he took the application and left the room. He came back after five long minutes—with the application *and* the gun and six brass-and-lead bullets. I glanced at the form. It was dated fifteen days earlier.

"The mail takes forever these days," he said. He lit a cigarette and winked.

I stood under a tree, conscious of the weight of the .38 in my bag. The only crowd in Central Park seemed to be around a street musician playing under a street lamp. No sign of Lupé or W.I.T.C.H. around Cleopatra's Needle—but what would *they* look like anyway?

I felt weak; my eyes weren't working right. Ten minutes went by. A chilly breeze picked up and blew up my skirt (the first one I'd worn in months) against my legs. I closed my eyes, blocking everything out, and leaned against a tree.

"Hi, Willis!" It was Lupé, right next to me. But when I

looked it wasn't. It was a white-haired Hispanic lady with a prominent, aquiline nose, bushy white brows, and bifocals.

"Lupé?"

"Yeah."

The old lady was wearing a jeweled W.I.T.C.H. symbol pinned to her bodice and a flashing light in a big transparent plastic diamond.

"You like it?" the old lady said. "It reacts to and is synchronized with the heartbeat."

"Are you Lupé?" I asked again. "You don't look like Lupé."

"It's a wig," she said, "and a putty nose and stuff. We got some theatrical makeup. One of the group is an actress. She's well known like a few others here; they don't want to be recognized."

She took my arm and walked me toward the Needle. Suddenly I saw all the other W.I.T.C.H. members. I hadn't noticed them before because they looked old, and how often do we notice the old? Old women in shapeless coats and babushkas came out from under the trees, got up from benches. Others were dressed more stylishly, in furs and hats—all with wizened faces and shuffling feet, bent backs. Only the eyes looked youthful: sharp and searching—and the *feet*; they wore sneakers and trendy running shoes. One of them, in a long cape, was passing out more of the diamond heart-lights. The others (maybe fifteen or so) stood in groups of three or four, talking softly.

The woman in the cape approached me with a heart-light.

"Take it, Willis," said Lupé, "you'll need it later tonight."

The other women were clustering around. "Do you want me to introduce you?" asked Lupé. "Or do you want to remain anonymous?"

"Introduce me, I guess."

"This is Willis Digby, everybody. Letters Editor at SIS."

There were murmurs of greeting, then some positive comments about the change in Letters. I noticed my heart-light, pinned to my lapel like a lavaliere mike, begin to flash quickly as my heart sped up. Praise. All the old ladies smiled. I reached in my bag, put on my rabbit ears, waved.

"I'll tell you everyone who's here later," said Lupé, "after you see what we're going to do. Maybe you'll enjoy it and want to come out on a run again."

The wind picked up again suddenly, blowing dead leaves everywhere. The moon chinned itself on the treetops.

"It's like Halloween," Lupé said. "We go out every so often and 'trick' somebody who deserves it, man or woman. This week, for example, we're going to settle a little score with Bob Hargill. Do you watch TV?"

"Not much. But I know who *he* is."

Bob Hargill was the guy who told his female newscaster partner that she was getting too old to sit beside him and cast the news. He'd said that he needed a young, more personally appealing woman by his side or it spoiled the "psychology" of the TV relationship. "I don't relate well to dogs," he'd said off the record, but apparently not far enough off.

We ran out on 81st Street—the moon was full up now. We ran loosely, like a pack of domesticated horses, debridled and set free on the plains. We gradually picked up speed, if not a collective sense of direction.

The .38 bounced along in my Danish schoolbag. "What are we going to do to Bob Hargill?" I asked the woman running next to me, who looked like Ronald McDonald's mom.

"We're not going to *do* anything to him—we're attempting to alter his thinking a little." She winked at me. "He's having dinner tonight at Capistrano. We're going to introduce ourselves to him."

Later, we were running down Lex, a flying squadron. The

gun jostled me. I felt faint but vaguely satisfied—running in a pack of old women in a big city will do that for you.

When we got close to the restaurant, we slowed down and huddled like the New York Jets Retirement League.

"We're going to do it the same way we did it to Norman Mailer," Lupé said. "Digby, just look involved. You'll see what to do."

The maître d' greeted us just inside the door of the restaurant.

He stared at the firefly diamonds. I noticed that many of the Witches' hearts were beating fast; the lights flashed like strobes. Lupé's blinked slowly, steadily, a beacon.

"We're Hot Flash, the singing telegram service made up almost exclusively of seniors!" Lupé sang out, with a quick look at me. The maître d' pursed his lips, tight as a stitch. One of his eyebrows jumped, stilled, jumped.

"Mr. Hargill is celebrating something special tonight, and this telegram is from his *mother*. We know he's in one of the private rooms here—may we quickly deliver our little message to him?"

"I will mention to him that you're here. The name again?"

Lupé put a hand on his arm. I saw a twenty peeping between her fingers. "Oh, *noooo*," she said. "That would ruin everything. You *can't* tell him we're here. It's a *singing* telegram—a *surprise!*" She gestured toward her elderly crew, and we all smiled. Someone curtsied. "From his mom," she repeated softly. She looked sweetly into the man's face. He looked the tiniest bit irritated that he was giving in—I thought I caught him glaring at my rabbit ears—but he pocketed the money and nodded, stepped aside. He turned his attention to a busy table, throwing over his shoulder, "He is in the far-right rear dining chamber. I'll find a waiter to escort you."

Instead of waiting for the waiter, we moved en masse in

the direction of the private dining rooms. I saw Lupé pulling a Minolta out of her pocket. We rumbled past low, elegant tables with flickering candles, banquettes for two, around a fountain, a heavy velvet curtain, rooms of seductive dining scenes, then into the final chamber.

I was last in, but I caught a glimpse of the famous Bob Hargill, touched up by the intimate lighting: ruddy-faced, his hair blown into stiff peaks like egg whites. He looked mildly affronted but not alarmed. A take-charge guy. His dining companion, a young woman in a sequined, low-cut camisole, put down her gleaming escargot tools, fork and vise. She whispered in his ear.

I caught part of what Lupé was announcing in a stage voice, facing Hargill.

". . . a singing telegram for you, Mr. Hargill. . . . Your recent comments about women and age. . . . These women are Witches. . . . Women's International Terrorist Conspiracy from Hell . . ."

Suddenly everyone around me went into position. I knew what it felt like to be caught onstage in the middle of a Broadway musical. The Witches began circling, doing a soft-shoe.

Hey, Bob, listen, Bob, women are great
(Even *after* thirty-eight!)
Even after *fifty-eight*, Bob—
It's amazing, they can still do the job!

Bob had heard enough already. He tried to get up, but a big old woman in a gray wig-hat kept an iron grip on his shoulder. His date started to smirk. He drank some wine, refilled his glass. He was shaking his head, scornful. He put a protective arm around his companion. She pulled away slightly.

I noticed one of the really ancient women doing a slow bump and grind in Bob's direction.

> At sixty-two, Bob, a woman's still strong—
> but statistics will tell you, something's wrong
> with the *guys:* they don't live very long!
> They're fragile, it seems, and weak—
> while a woman is, let's see, at her sexual peak:
> who knows *when,* Bob?????
> But you've made some guesses. . . .

The ancient woman gave one last pelvic grind, tossed aside her cane, then sprang suddenly, agilely, for Hargill's head. The date jumped away. There was a tremendous tussle. He grabbed his head and held on for dear life. The old woman pulled hard, grunting. She looked like a mad brain surgeon. I moved in closer, to get a better look. Then there was a triumphant shriek, the old lady brandished a wavy chunk of Bob's scalp. She waved the shag of fake-blond hair above her head. Lupé's flash attachment framed them again and again—I was blinded temporarily.

> Bye, Bob, bye—
> you'll see us in your dreams.
> You'll never know a Witch
> from a Bimbo now—
> (she isn't what she seems!)

A waiter rushed in, then another. One shouted in Spanish and Lupé answered him, *"Besame colo!"* Bob Hargill's bald pate, naked as a sexual organ, drew everyone's eyes. He was thrashing around in his seat, shouting incoherently, trying to detain the old broad who'd dehaired him, but Lupé came up from behind and released his hold with a quick karate chop. Bob's date looked as if she were about to wet her pants. In the middle of everything, she pulled the wine bottle out of its ice cradle and poured herself another glass. We began moving rapidly out the door—I thought I caught a wink pass between her and Lupé—or did I imagine it?

We broke ranks now, running pell-mell—I wasn't jogging too fast, however, to miss Terence Major and his beautiful co-star in the play *Blind or Sightless?* (or whatever it was) having a romantic little dinner.

He stared, openmouthed, as I ran past, following the herd of grandmothers in Nikes and flashers. It did not seem entirely out-of-mood for me to thumb my nose at him.

At the door the maître d' was wrestling a Witch to the floor—she was striking feebly at him with her walking stick. Lupé was having some trouble extricating her—customers were getting in the way, shouting at the maître d' to leave the old woman alone. In the general confusion someone pushed me hard from behind, and I staggered forward. My bag slumped off my shoulder and the .38 slid to the floor. The maitre d' saw it and jumped away like a kid on a pogo stick.

"They're armed!" he cried in a strangled voice.

Everyone drew away from me, silent, as I picked the gun up and slipped it back in my bag.

"Let's go!" Lupé snarled, and we went.

"Jesus, Digby," she panted, after we'd run about forty blocks. Everyone stood under a tree in the Park pulling off noses and wigs, laughing hysterically as breath came back, slapping palms.

"Why are you carrying a piece?"

The Witches were doing imitations of Hargill, the struggle, his face as his hair came off. The ancient attacker, transformed into a person I recognized from TV, a news anchor, held up the toupee like a scalp, whooped, and did a war dance. Then she got into a cab and disappeared. I thought I saw Betty Berry in white hair and glasses, smoking a cigarette. I wanted suddenly to run over and hug her, but the moment was lost.

"Why do *you* carry a camera?"

"Evidence. Blackmail. Yuks. Whatever. *This* one we'll mail into the *News* anonymously—we have a Witch on the inside there. She'll run it with an appropriate caption."

I shook her hand. "Thanks for asking me, Lupé. I haven't had such a good time in years."

Lupé smiled enigmatically. "Why you carryin' it?"

I stopped smiling. "You know that letter I printed? From the crazy guy?"

I decided to sleep at my mother's apartment. She had a place on York and 66th she'd kept since my father died. She also had a house on the beach in Carmel, where she spent most of the year. But she couldn't quite give up New York. I felt a little guilty about pretending that I wanted to see her—but I couldn't tell her about The Watcher. She would have begun by putting the National Guard on alert.

I came in, offering the heart-light as a little gift (she loved to jog and it was a great pulse monitor), chattering on about my busy schedule. It turned out that she was preoccupied. She'd taken up painting the last few years, and a gallery in Carmel had mounted a show of her work along with that of four other local artists. A month ago the gallery had been broken into and paintings by every one of the artists except her had been stolen.

"That's what I just can't fathom," she said, sipping her decaf from a *Cats* mug. "They were *systematic* about rejecting my work. They'd pull three paintings in a row off the wall, then they'd leave one of mine. Take four more, leave mine.

It was an absolutely critical reaction. Do you know how the local papers put it? *'Left behind* was work by Eleanor Digby . . .' How do you think I feel, Willis?"

"Not good, Mom," I said. I was trying to find something in the refrigerator to eat. Everything was Weight Watchers. Finally I settled on some low-fat cream cheese and crispbread.

"Did they catch the guys who did it?" I wanted to keep her on the subject; otherwise the conversation could take a dangerous lurch in the direction of Terence.

She frowned. I hadn't looked up from my sandwich, but I knew she was frowning—she knew me well enough to have recognized the feigned interest in my voice. Like all mothers, though, she took what interest she could get.

"Who knows?" she snorted. "I flew East to nurse my ego."

She sighed and stared morosely through the kitchen door to the living room wall where a painting of me at four hung. She'd taken it from a photograph; I was naked at the beach, holding a sand bucket in one hand, scratching my left buttock with the other. Next to it hung a painting of a beachcomber with a walrus mustache. The colors were brilliant, but the sense of proportion was just a little off in each one. I loved them.

"The thieves had no taste, Mom," I said.

She smiled ruefully. "Thanks dear. Now. Have you seen Terence?"

Twelve

The next morning I went out (scorning my mother's breakfast of Weight Watchers' granola and low-fat yogurt) and bought the papers, some Danish, and espresso. Mom had gone out jogging along the river with a friend—another over-sixty in peak condition.

I unlocked her door, panting, after sprinting up five flights, just to prove to myself I could breathe heavily, and dropped the papers on the entry tiles. A headline: BROOK-HEART SCANDAL, blah, blah—my name leaped out at me. Holly *had* given them some info yesterday:

Willis Digby, editor at SISTERHOOD magazine, first contacted the *Mirror* with information sent to her by Iris Moss, a patient at Brookheart. In a letter to Ms. Digby, Ms. Moss described herself as a rape victim and named a staff member as the perpetrator. Ms. Digby approached the city desk with these facts, which led to the *Mirror* investigation . . .

The phone rang. It was Terence.

"I *thought* you might be there! I called your apartment about ten times last night. What are you doing at your mom's?"

"Avoiding a guy."

"Oh."

"A guy who wants to kill me. I'll tell you about it later."

There was a pause. "Is he one of those wackos you get letters from? I saw the thing in the paper—"

"Yeah." I cut him off wearily. "Listen . . ."

"Speaking of wackos, Willis, do you mind my asking what you were doing running through Capistrano last night with that big gang of . . . grannies, ripping off Bob Hargill's toupee and threatening the maître d'?"

"Nobody threatened the maître d'."

"He said the one with the blond hair—the only terrorist under seventy, he said. You were the one who kinda fit the description."

I didn't respond.

"He said you pointed a gun at him."

"That's a lie. The gun fell out of my bag."

"What gun? What the hell are you doing with a gun?"

"To protect myself from the guy who wants to kill me. Aren't you listening?"

He asked to see me, he said it sounded like we needed to talk. I wouldn't mind, I said, having someone with me when I went back to the apartment.

I decided to take the morning off, and we met at the Plaza fountain. He looked worried. He kept stealing glances at me, as if I were about to put on a pinwheel beanie and swallow fire. The worst part of it was—he looked sorry for me.

The night before I had leaned over to my mother, who was seated in front of the TV doing isometrics. I asked her if she thought I was crazy. I mean, I'd said, had she ever noticed when I was a kid, any signs of *real* instability?

She shook her wrists free of invisible shackles and turned to answer me in characteristic fashion, with a non sequitur, an anecdote from my childhood. Talking to her was something like studying with a Zen master. You got answers but you never knew until later what their connection to your question was.

"You were such a strange baby," she mused. She brushed a strand of hair out of my eyes awkwardly, with the back of her hand. "You didn't talk for the longest time—you were like a *meat loaf:* no 'mama,' no 'dada,' no 'bye-bye.' I was beginning to worry—you were two and a half, I think. I took you to Dr. Townsend—remember him?—and he said, 'Don't worry, Mrs. Digby, she'll talk up a storm when she's ready to!' Boy, was he *right.* You were sitting in your high chair late one afternoon. . . ." I smiled at her, trying to look interested, but I'd heard this story about four hundred times.

"I was feeding you some typically disgusting baby food—strained peas, I think. The peas were very hot. I put them down steaming in front of you, and then I started to daydream, you know, just kind of drifted off, with a spoonful of this stuff suspended in the air between us. You got this very annoyed look on your face—I'll never forget it. Then you nodded at the spoonful of peas. 'Blow on it, dummy!' you said."

She laughed helplessly; tears came to her eyes. She patted my hands and shook her head. I chuckled a little, trying hard, but I'd lip-synched the punch line with her, and anyway, the story had always made me a little nervous. Now I wondered: Did this precocious wise-cracking indicate the first signs of juvenile dementia?

She saw my expression finally. "You're *not* crazy," she said emphatically and patted my hand again. Then I saw her face change, darken. I heard her voice, in memory, behind the door of the bedroom, berating my father, who sat staring into space, a drink in his hands. "Whose fault was it?" the voice, hers, asked. I remember pushing open the door. She wore a satin dressing gown and her hair was piled on top of her head. I thought she looked beautiful, but her expression frightened me. "Are you all right?" she asked me, looking terrified, as if she'd seen a ghost. Something in her tone, I remember, made me think that I was *not*. Her voice went too high at the end of the question, and she didn't seem to really want an answer. *She's afraid of me*, I remember thinking. *She thinks I'm a crazy person, a murderer. She's not sure what to do.* I looked past her to my father, sitting (so unlike him!) slumped at the edge of the bed, his feet on the floor, head in his hands. A bottle of Jack Daniel's lit red gold from behind by the night-table lamp. On the wall the family pictures: Mom's watercolors, a framed newspaper photo of Dad and me in hunting clothes, holding up our booty.

"Dad?"

He glanced up at me—his eyes were surprisingly clear—but his words were slurred. "It's okay, Willis, it's all okay. It's all taken care of. Go to bed now."

I remember asking *what*, what had been taken care of.

He turned away from me.

"Eleanor," he said, "tell her to get to bed now. Shut the door."

She came to the door and looked down at me for a minute.

"Go to sleep now, Willis," she said. "You need to sleep." She shut the door in my face.

I wondered if she was remembering this too. "You're *not* crazy," she said again. "You're thinking about that Matthew Kallam thing, aren't you? Well, I can tell you my feeling about *that*. Your father whisked it all away at the time; he forbade me to mention it to you ever again. So we just let it go. But there it *is*, still on your mind, after all these years, of course. As I told him it would be."

She laughed ruefully and shook her head. "It was an accident, that's all. A tragic, tragic happening, but an accident all the same. And the way your father raised you, Willis, to be a kind of . . . smart-ass—that was an accident too. All wrong. He needed a son to make a smart-ass of."

"So *that's* what's wrong with me? I'm a smart-ass?"

I saw her again in her satin dressing gown, the fear in her face as she looked at me. Then I saw myself rushing in the door, sixth grade; we were stationed at Schofield that year: we had a gorgeous tacky house with a lanai covered with vines, a vine *roof*, those tiny geckos crawling on the walls, ceiling fans—I was in heaven. I ran in with my report card, *straight A's!* I called—and she hugged me. She was brown from the sun, and she had my favorite perfume on, *La De*, and when I hugged her tighter (I couldn't stop myself, I just couldn't let her go), she pulled away. I held on grimly. It was almost a polite struggle. She laughed nervously and pulled away with force, smiling at me.

Now she winked and got up to adjust the color. I watched her kneel in front of the set. She turned and showed me her profile, pouty, full-lipped, pixieish in her sixty-first year, framed by the twenty-one-inch head of Dan Rather. A gold scalloped earring flashed.

She threw the comment over her shoulder: "You just don't let people love you."

It was a cold sunny day; the breeze batted fountain water on us.

"I'm *not* crazy," I said, echoing my mother.

Terence didn't look convinced.

"Who *were* all those old ladies last night? Friends of your mom's?"

I asked him to forget about the night before. I'd bigger troubles than that, I told him. I gave him a capsule description of The Watcher. I asked him to accompany me down to my apartment. I was scared, I told him. What I didn't say was that I wanted to be with him again.

He put his arms around me. "Willis, if you're in trouble, I'm here."

For once I said nothing, though I had to K.O. and straitjacket my tongue. We sat a long time holding each other. Then we got up, hailed a cab, and sped down Fifth.

In my apartment the sun was blinding. We sat having coffee in the tiny kitchen. Nothing that had happened yesterday seemed real: The Watcher, W.I.T.C.H., the .38 still smoldering in my book bag. Sunlight leaped from the chrome pots and pans hanging from a metal hoop and dazzled a row of glass spice jars. My neighbor, the would-be opera singer, fractured his scales. *Ti do ti.*

I found that I could not refer to our separation and impending divorce. Terence seemed reluctant to bring the subject up too. Before long we were holding each other again and walking to the bedroom. My platform bed waited, a low altar.

No bogeyman in there. Just whatever we had to fear from each other, after we pulled the shades, which turned out at the moment to be nothing. At the moment it turned out that we wished each other well; in fact, wished each other intense joy and pleasure. We seemed to want to forgive each other, if that's what the sobbing and caressing, the cries to God, and the long very specific silences were all about. We made love and then we lay quietly, listening to the opera singer.

"I don't know how to say this. . . ." he began, thereby saying everything.

"You want to tell me that you're sorry about the miscarriage."

He looked at me, worriedly. "Yes. Couldn't you let

Carol Muske-Dukes

120

me say it? I never got a chance to really tell you how I felt until now."

I had a little newsreel I ran in my head. It featured me and my unborn child. The newsreel was the old Movietone variety; the voice-over quavered with mock portentousness. It seemed I was in the news, because I was a medical aberration—the child in my womb could talk to me.

I demonstrated this phenomenon for the camera by placing a microphone on my huge belly.

"Are you there?" I asked in a soft voice. "Are you there?"

"Yes," answered an eerie, flutelike voice. "Take that thing away."

The miracle was, my kid and I had long dialogues about life as I lay in bed, touching my belly. I made the cameras disappear from my reverie, but the grainy newsreel background remained. I saw myself, lying there, talking with my child.

"It's a very strange world," I told her. "You might not like it when you come out."

There was a pause. Then the eerie flutevoice. "I have to come *out*?"

I looked over at Terence. This was not the kind of imagery one could easily paint, postcoitus. But the daydream had been around for some time—came and went, got longer and more complex. The unborn child, Lily, said wondrous things to me. Like Tracy St. Martin, the woman I'd called up that night, I talked to my womb.

I began to cry. And Terence, as the script demanded, was tender, compassionate, comforting. He put his arms around me, he held my head against his heart. But did I believe he knew what I felt, what shadows I saw moving on the shade? He was a man who'd just made love to a woman, soon to be smoothing his mussed hair and checking his Rolex. Deep inside he thought the tears were flattering; he thought the tears were for him.

I sat up. "Terence, I have a sort of fantasy. I fantasize that I am still carrying a child, that she has a name and I can talk to her. I mean—I talk to her and she answers me. Her name is Lily. She tells me all kinds of things: what a heartbeat sounds like on the *inside*, how she can tell if I'm deep asleep or when I wake up. . . . I tell her about life *outside*, what the subway is, why it's so noisy, what happens when I'm startled, what sunlight looks like, and I've tried to explain *touch*. You see, that's a hard one for someone in the womb to follow. . . ." I began to cry again.

Terence, who had been looking at me in astonishment, then did a wonderful thing. He slid down my body and put his mouth against my belly.

"Lily," he said. "Lily, Willis. Lily. Do you feel this? Do you both feel this? This is *touch*." And he kissed my stomach.

After a long time we got up. He checked the door locks and secured all the windows. I didn't mind any of this show of male protectiveness. For one thing, though it made me nervous, it had a short shelf life (who can be protective *all* the time?) and I knew it made him feel good. Why shouldn't one of us feel good? I personally felt that an attack dog and twelve precinct alarms couldn't keep this guy out. And I knew I had to face this on my own. But I didn't say that.

We put in a call to Detective Blair, who was out, but whose secretary swore he'd call back. Terence even offered to talk to Whizzer the doorman, impress on him the need for vigilance.

He asked to see the .38, turned it solemnly over and over in his hands.

"I don't like you carrying this," he said. "It makes me very nervous."

"It makes *me* a lot more nervous that this guy wants to cut me up in tiny pieces and serve me at Benihana."

He handed the gun back.

Carol Muske-Dukes

122

"Your letters column has become a personal ad for your self-destructiveness. An 'I dare you' to the world."

"That's what I need right now. A little armchair psychology. It may interest you to know, Herr Doktor, that I am, even as we speak, later for an interview with someone from the *Mirror* who thinks that my letters column recently did a great deal of social good. Self-destructive as it may be."

Terence stopped me at the door. "It would be great if we didn't ruin things now." He kissed me. I believed suddenly that he cared about me. It happened just like that. And it was not due to his careful lack of theatricality or my own nostalgia for our shared past. It was simply that when I looked at him, he looked straight back at me. He looked exhausted suddenly and ordinary, somebody concerned and pained. His appropriation of my suffering was *familial:* I recognized the feeling and returned it. It was as if everything about our relationship had acquired a weariness that was good, almost languorous, surprising in its sexual and familial irony. We had been *hurt* together.

He put on his jacket and followed me into the elevator. As I stepped out into the street, he remained in the lobby, talking earnestly to Whizzer the doorman, one hand on the older guy's gold-braided shoulder.

"But why would you believe the things said in a letter from an inmate of an insane asylum?"

My interviewer was trying to get me to admit something. I wasn't sure what. She was up against a real deadline: She'd been told she had to deliver my interview for a half-page inset for the following day. She was a tough cookie and I work at the tough cookie bakery. This one was a mean macaroon. Not only that, she was actually wearing a pink mohair suit, an article of clothing I had previously thought existed only in "Benny and the Jets."

I smiled back at her. I explained to her how I had come

to answer the crazy mail, how I had come to take it seriously. I showed her the rabbit ears. She looked at them, then looked at me awhile, then started scribbling furiously.

"I've also been feeling a bit 'out of sync' myself," I said. "If you feel vulnerable, you're more open to the vulnerable. I always loved the idea Richard Brautigan had, of a library where rejected manuscripts could be cherished. Iris Moss's letter was strange, there's no doubt about that, but it was still a letter from *someone*, a message, in this case a plea for help."

"When you wear those . . . ears, you feel closer to your correspondents?"

I put the ears on and the photographer who'd accompanied her started shooting. I saw Page, out of the corner of my eye, holding an imaginary gun to her head.

"I feel like a radio tower. . . . I pull everybody in."

That night as I lay in bed at Page's, listening to her singing Springsteen in the shower, Lily spoke to me again.

"I liked that dream you had last night" she said, "the one where we're in the beautiful warm place?"

"Oh yeah . . . the South Seas," I said. "I remember that dream now, it was *heavenly*. We were in Tahiti; I was carrying you inside me, with a *gigantic* belly, walking on warm white sand at sunset. The water was orchid-colored. The *sky* was orchid-colored."

"Heavenly," she said. Then, after a while, primly: "But there were boats, bad boats on the water."

"Warships. But they didn't hurt us—they just floated there. They didn't hurt us."

"You walked away down the beach. I could feel you looking toward the light. You were not afraid."

"The sun was setting. Turning the water blood-colored. But nothing could hurt us."

"We were safe" said Lily. "Safe."

Thirteen

Dear Letters Editor,

Well! I'm Bea Plotkin and I have some socko news that I *know* you'll be interested in. I've written to you many times before from my residence here in Utah, but apparently my letters did not get through to you.

You are absolutely right, gals, when you say you gals are equal to the guys. I'm rootin' for you! You see, I am the Light of the World and I am a gal. I'm the Savior, I'm god. The reason I didn't put any caps there on god, you see, gals, is because *she* is now equal to *he*—and to everyone else in the whole cotton-pickin' human race! Isn't that a scorch?

I know that this is a bit hard to take in, but if you care about the women's lib movement enough, *CHECK IT OUT!* Because here's the clincher: Can you believe that they have me in a hospital here in Skyhigh, Utah, because they are in awe of me, they can't quite believe that I am who I say I am?! Oh, the tiny, tiny little minnow-minds of them—of wee little faith! god said if you read Chapter 23 of Jeremiah in the King James version of the Bible—he was going to send down another lord. Well, change that he to she, then the lord is *me*, Lordess of All Light: Bea! Think about it—three letters in god, three in Bea! Please send someone *now* to assist in my release, so we can get this dog-and-pony show on the road here!

Blessings on ya, gals!
Bea

I scribbled on a SIS pad. There were six letters in Willis . . . and seven in "eggroll." I put Bea's tenth letter aside.

A handwritten note, no stamp, stuck in with the rest. I recognized the script at once.

Willis,
    I missed you last night. I wanted so much to see you. I wanted to explain everything to you. I know when you meet me you'll listen to me. Zero hour is coming, Willis. Please don't be afraid.

The Watcher

I ran, with the note in my hand, to Minnie W-W-G's reception desk.

"How did this get in my mail, Minnie? Did you see anybody putting something in one of the bags?"

"Noooo . . . listen, Willis, my fiancé and I are thinking of *baby* names!! Do you still have that list I gave you before you had that . . . miscarriage? I *know* it's jumping the gun a little, but with our hyphen problems—"

"Minnie. *Shut up.* Concentrate. Did you see anyone hanging around the lobby, my desk, the elevators? This is *important!*"

"Willis, I *told* you—I haven't seen *anyone.* Please don't take that tone with me. I have a *job* to do here, you know."

She turned away, pouting.

I asked the elevator operator—he remembered nothing. Either this guy was Mr. Wallpaper or he was dressed up as a janitor—or a mailman. I considered briefly the idea that Nathan Grapes, the 210-pound mailman, was The Watcher, but discarded it.

Page looked at The Watcher's note. Her round sweet face looked distressed. "If you take those goddamn ears off, you can come and stay with me tonight."

I started to say no, then I thought of my apartment, of trying to sleep in my bed alone.

"Thanks, Page."

Lupé strolled over. She looked like herself again in her overalls and black lipstick and Afro.

"Don't worry, Willis," she said. "One of the Witches lives near your apartment—she walks her pit bull right in front of your building. *She'll* let our network know if some bozo is hangin' around."

The next morning Page and I picked up papers at the 72nd Street newsstand on our way to SIS.

I was featured in both the *News* and the *Mirror.* In the *News* there was the piece, as promised, on Bob Hargill—a photograph with the caption:

GUN-TOTING GRANNIES "SCALP" HARGILL

"I'm 72 and I look better than him,"
wrinkled "rug" robber retorts!

There was a large photograph of Hargill's hair hijack, and there *I* was, looking stupid in the background; the rabbit ears sticking up like bright ideas. One had only to glance to the front page of the other paper, "Exclusive to the New York *Mirror*," an inset box with a photograph of me, again with the rabbit ears on, to make a basic connection.

"Jesus," said Page, making the connection, "what are you doing to Bob Hargill here? And look at those ridiculous rabbit ears *again*! Aren't you embarrassed by this stuff?"

I was not, in fact, embarrassed. I was terrified that I would be charged with Forcible Hair Removal or something, but not embarrassed. The *News* made mention of a "young (compared to the others) blond terrorist in Bugs Bunny ears, who seemed, except for carrying a firearm, to be along for the ride." The *Mirror* interview, as I sped-read through it, simply made me sound like an asshole. In fact, Penny Wall, the *Mirror* reporter, had with unexpected clemency made me sound like a somewhat charming asshole.

Under the headline:

SIS EDITOR WITH "CRAZY" SPIRIT
CHANGES THE "LETTER" OF THE LAW

she had written the following:

Sitting at her bright red desk piled high with mail from all over the U.S. and Canada and everywhere SISTERHOOD magazine is sold is Letters Editor Willis Jane Digby. Ms. Digby is wearing (besides a pixilated gleam in her large green eyes) a tuxedo jacket and jeans *and* a pair of rabbit ears on her head. Her bizarre attire underscores her recent personal campaign to redefine what people mean by "crazy."

Not long ago Ms. Digby began using her bimonthly column to print (often insulting) personal responses to selected correspondents—in a kind of mean-ingenuous, feminist-Will Rogers style. On the other hand, she began to pay closer attention to what her more unlikely correspondents were actually *saying*.

Last week Editor Digby tipped the *Mirror* off to apparently widespread sexual abuse of patients of Brookheart State Hospital by staff members. She received information about the situation at Brookheart from a letter that would have been tossed into the "circular file" by most editors, after a bemused reading. The letter, from a patient at Brookheart, read, in effect, like a communication from a "crazy person." The letter's style was verbose and wandering, with insistent, recurring accusations about "hypnosis" and "seminal fluid."

Ms. Digby says: "Most people never write *any*thing anymore. The act of writing is an exotic occupation. The act of writing one's opinions on paper and sending them out for publication is even more exotic. It's an occasion. I try to honor that occasion. I try not to publish just the editorial bread-and-butter letters one sees in most magazine columns. A fellow SIS editor, Betty Berry, made me realize that just being flippant worked for some correspondents—for others, it was necessary to have a heart.

"In the main, I get two types of 'crazy' letters. I get the ordinary person who sounds crazy, is fed up, and trying to make an outrageous, sarcastic point, *and* I get really disturbed or obsessed crazy individuals who are trying to sound ordinary, rational.

"I see my column as a kind of demilitarized zone where these two impulses—the desire of the sane to go crazy and the desire of the crazy to be sane—converge."

Editor Digby claims that in the case of the Brookheart resident (whose letter would fall into the latter category), something "leaped out at her" from between the lines; she "identified" with the patient's heroic attempt to communicate in her own "language." Then she met with the patient and was convinced. "Because SIS is a feminist magazine, we tend to attract more than the usual crowd of cranks and paranoiacs. But we also hear the legitimate voices of extremity, people pushed beyond the limit.

"I've learned to dive off the deep end into the subconscious of the Sex War. I've learned to scuba among predictable rhetorical undersea plant life and discover the authentic pearl, the real valuable produced by sexual friction. The letter from the Brookheart patient was a case in point."

The article ended by my "chirping" (as the reporter put it), "I'm crazy too!" and waving my rabbit ears.

This last made me feel like retching—which meant that my mother would be very proud. (*Until* she checked out the *News*, I recalled suddenly.) I felt dazed.

"Come on, Digby," said Page, "let's get you back in the ring."

The phone on my desk was ringing nonstop. Everybody from the mayor's office to "New York at Five" wanted to talk to me. Suddenly I was a weird kind of celebrity. The only two people I *hadn't* heard from were The Watcher and Bob Hargill—would he send a lawyer?

Holly was beside herself with joy. She hugged me again and again. "Willis, you've given SIS a vision! You've pointed out a new direction for us!" She paused and lowered her voice. "Willis. Marge showed me a photo in the *News* today with somebody who looks like you in the background of that shot of Bob Hargill. Is it you?"

Minnie, with her infallible sense of timing, galumphed up, flushed with importance. "It's PAPARAZZI magazine on the phone! They want to interview you for their next issue. They want to interview you in your apartment! You're *famous*, Willis! I told them tomorrow afternoon is okay, okay?? God, Willis, PAPARAZZI magazine!!" She grabbed my arms and shook me up and down. "Names!" she cried. "*Big* names!"

Holly gave her an icy look, took her arm, and escorted her back to her phones.

I flipped through the mail. There was a billet-doux from Dino, another hand-delivered item.

Hey Digby!

I see here in the *News* they done an article on you. What next? They gonna do one on Ideeya Mean? Hey your not a bad-lookin broad Digby. No tits but see if you can get a pair of big sillycone casabas made and I might give you a turn! By the way, its *still* hard!!!

Yours truly,

THE HUMAN POKER

(A.K.A. Dino)

I hadn't lost Holly. She sat down at my desk.

"What were you doing in that photo with Hargill, Willis?"

"I was out with W.I.T.C.H.," I said. "If you want to know more, go ask Lupé. Maybe she'll tell you. I'm not at liberty to say anything further, unfortunately."

"What if Hargill calls up? Or his legal people? Can you at least tell me why there was a gun?"

I sighed. "No, I can't. If I could, though, Holl, I really would."

I grubbed around inside my mailbags. She sat staring at me for a while, then got up and walked away.

The phone rang. It was Terence. "Come over tonight. After the show I'll make a fire and we can have a late dinner and an early bed. I promise I will ask *no* questions about what I've seen in the papers today."

Fourteen

Dear WJD,

As you know from my previous letters, I am OTRO CORPUS, electronic alien being. Most recently I have inhabited a small plastic tub of oleomargarine *and* Howard Cosell, to determine the broad parameters of your protoplasmic entities. Now I am devoting myself to research, which includes inhabiting world leaders.

I have *tried* to inhabit the President of the United States, with results unlike any achieved to date. It appears, after laboratory cultures and electronic data cross-indexing, that either the cerebral and rectal units are reversed, or the brain cavity has been altered by taxidermy, in effect "stuffed." We are getting severely foreshortened brain emissions similar in structure and duration to those given off in our own bioenvironment by a soil base roughly equivalent to your *Playdough.*

Carol Muske-Dukes

I flipped this one in my "Hold: Possible" pile and read on.

Dear Willis Digby,

I am a flight attendant on Trans-National Airlines, and I have to tell you that I think I am going crazy too. I've been reading the letters you printed and your answers to them, and I decided, like the woman who feeds her unwitting husband cat food every morning, that *everybody* should have a *crazy safety valve.*

I'm absolutely ecstatic when I tell you that without any change in cabin pressure, certain of my passengers are getting high on cocktails "on the rocks" that I serve up with just a weensy spritz of blue "freeze," a waste-disposal substance we use in the toilet unit. Just a crystal in every irritating bozo's drink . . . and I feel so much *better* about everything!

Hope to see you on a flight soon.

Bottoms up,
Anonymous Stew

I took the train from Grand Central, then a cab to Brook-heart. I had an old woman cabdriver who was in a big hurry to get me inside. I stared at her caved-in straw hat and the back of her grizzled neck. She was nearly *standing* on the accelerator.

"Hey," I called, "slow down. I'm not in that big a rush to get there!"

Her cagey old eyes appeared in the dash mirror. "You're a reporter, right?" She didn't wait for an answer. "There musta been a thousand of 'em around here last week. They all wanna get up there *fast!*" She cackled. "You're a little late, honey!"

"I'm not a reporter," I said. "I'm a friend of one of the residents."

The eyes blinked, disappointed. She slowed down.

"I wouldn't be in such a hurry then, if I were you," she said, half to herself.

We pulled in at the gates, the young guard slid off his Walkman just long enough to check my name off the visitors' list. A tiny, tinny Pat Benatar sang like a cricket around his neck as he signed a pass for me.

Brookheart was something of an architectural anomaly. Though it had been built in the late twenties or thirties, like so many other American fun houses, it lacked the usual fake Gothic façade. It looked instead like a monastery, like a photograph I'd once seen of St. Remy, the insane asylum where Vincent Van Gogh spent his last days painting and where he finally killed himself. It had two long, low wings extending from a center, an imposing front with a stone circular pool on the main lawn. It looked escape-proof, but wasn't, due to its much-vaunted liberality: no locks, no bars. This policy had left its inmates unprotected from internal corruption—that is to say, unprotected from the sane.

"Hello!" called Iris, poking her head into the Reception Area, where I sat reading *Psychology Quarterly*. I was shocked again by her physical appearance. Her rolling eye seemed more anchored today, but her stitched-up face and skull looked as raw as recent suturing. A surviving victim of the Texas Chain Saw Massacre.

She wore a bright green shiny taffeta dress; her rigid prosthetic fingers plucked at it nervously.

"Hi there," I said, shaking the plastic hand. "Iris. You're famous, kid."

"So are you!" she shouted. "You and me, Digby! You and me!!" The eye rolled back in her head.

She snapped her fingers. "It's gone," she whispered,

"gone! All rampant seminal fluid on the premises! It's *evaporated!*" Her strange speech impediment grew more pronounced. She said "e-val-porated."

She sat in one of the ugly naugahyde chairs and bounced up and down. "Reporters have been coming and going, going and coming. They indicted the Spiders, the guys who pull the strings at the top! They found Basil Schrantz, trying to run to *California.* . . ."

"You," I said, "you did it all. You wrote the letter that brought the empire down."

"Yeah," she said, glancing around furtively, "but *now* somebody, I'm not sure *who* yet, is smearing Tiger Balm on each and every sanitary napkin in the washrooms!"

"Let's talk about it later, okay? Can we go see the Crafts Fair now?"

The crafts filled a few long steel tables in the Day Room, a big windowless space with dull overhead lights. The unindicted nurses and attendants kept a discreet distance from the patients manning the tables, coming forward occasionally to pull a fist gently from a drooling mouth or to help make change or take someone to the bathroom.

There were painted ceramics and hand-thrown pottery bowls and clay ashtrays and bowlegged clay horses and many-legged clay octupi. There were bead earrings and bangles and colored fish mobiles and woven baskets. Then there were the products of altered visual imaginations: a plaster-of-Paris gnome with a huge erection, a Tina Turner scrub brush, a clay tarantula with a Groucho Marx face and cigar, a hardened Playdough Jesus on a trapeze, swinging by one leg, an arm raised in casual blessing. There was a sampler that read: STICK A VITAMIN IN YOUR EYE in shaky script, and blue knit infant booties, size 9, and a tea cozy that said "Butt Out." Iris showed me the pairs of underpants she'd personally tie-dyed.

"The investigators wanted to keep only a *few* of these for evidence," she confided. "The rest I made Art of." She paused and looked levelly at me. "I washed them first."

I bought the "Butt Out" tea cozy and an ashtray that said "Camomile Smile." "Those are Dolly Winkey's," said Iris. "She gets thing reversed." I bought a pair of Iris's pants, as a memento. I really wanted the trapeze Jesus, but the mother of the young man who had made it picked it up and held it to her heart, protectively.

At the last minute I picked up an Empire State Building made of bits of wire soldered together. I wondered where the artist got *wire* (the Electric Shock Room?), but I didn't ask Iris. The spire was sharp as a hypodermic. Iris saw it in my hand. "They only allowed one of those to be made," she whispered as I bought it. "Dalbert kept trying to clean his ears with it."

We moved along the tables, looking at the wares. "We expected a real crowd," said Iris sadly. "We thought all the recent publicity would be good for business. But people rushed up here for two or three days—then *poof!*"

A group of patients, mostly women, mostly shapeless and ageless, dressed in civvies (carefully buttoned shirts and dresses and out-of-date pants, bell-bottoms and floral prints), stood by, pointing and smiling, whispering among themselves. A dwarfish girl with a huge brow she'd tried to cover ineffectually with bangs had a very loud case of hiccups. Another, a camel-faced woman with long red stringy hair and a Hawaiian shirt, stared at everyone and repeated, "Short form! Use the short form!" in a commanding tone.

Yet another, young and mongoloid-looking, very fat, stepped away from the crowd of patients, hurried over to me, and kissed me very softly on the cheek.

"Thank you," I murmured, touched. She kissed me again. And again. Her eyes were huge and brown.

"That's enough now, Nina," said Iris. She gently disengaged the girl and pushed her toward a refreshment table. Nina began walking away but turned back.

"Hey," she called after us. *"Hey,* you!"

We picked up some Cokes and piled chocolate chip cookies on paper plates and went outside to sit under a tree. I threw my bag carelessly on the ground. I'd remembered at the last minute to remove the .38 on a pit stop at my apartment. I'd been right about the metal detector and the security guard. Besides, carrying a gun was making me too nervous.

The "grounds" stretched around us, about half an acre of what I call Bronx grass: hybrid of yellow-green bald spots, bottle caps, gum wrappers, and some stunted vegetation.

Iris wolfed her cookies, then looked at mine. I pushed them toward her.

"What's wrong?" she asked. "You're not hungry." (She said hung-ly.)

"Iris, there's somebody who wants to kill me. He's following me."

Her jaws stopped working; she stared at me.

"At first he was just trying to scare me, I think. Then I published one of his letters to me and he got really angry. Now he's after me."

I told her about the note on my door and the note at SIS—how he seemed to be able to get in anywhere.

"I got a gun. *And* I've been staying with friends at night. But I can't do that forever. I'm going home tonight and I'm going to stay there, no matter *what* happens."

Iris started chewing again.

"Where is the gun now?"

"I left it in my apartment—in the drawer of the night table next to the bed. I'm not going to carry it around anymore. I don't like it."

Iris polished off the last cookie. She drank some Coke and burped an enormous burp.

"Kill 'em." She belched.

"Huh?"

"Kill the rat-head, the bag of seminal fluid. Blow him into New Jersey."

"Iris. There's something else I have to tell you. I did that once to someone. When I was a kid. It was an accident, but nonetheless I did it. It's made me crazy. But"—I leaned closer to her—"what I can't understand about myself is *as soon* as this guy started bugging me, I wanted a gun. I went out and got a gun. Why? Now I can't sleep at all. I keep seeing the face of . . . Matthew, the kid I shot. Then I keep dreaming of this gun I'm carrying. I dreamed I was carrying it wrapped up like a baby. Then I talk to a baby that I lost some months ago, as if she were still in my *womb*. Her name is Lily, Iris."

Iris nodded and belched again, a long, low, grieving expulsion of air. She had eaten all the cookies and had drunk both Cokes. Her face was so chopped up it was hard to read; it did not organize readily into identifiable expressions. Now was no exception, but then I saw a tear slowly form at the edge of her jumping eye.

"Babies and guns"—she burped again—"that's America. You were having a patriotic dream." She sat up a little, reached over and touched my hand. "If anybody hurts you, I'll kill them," she said. "If anyone touches you when I'm not there, *you* kill them for me. What happened to you before, shooting the kid, that was an accident. *I* had an accident too. I had an accident and I was *exploded*."

She brought her face close to mine, brushed the tear away. "I was exploded, and my heart stopped three times. They wanted to pronounce me dead three times, the doctor told me afterward. There were *pieces* of me, an arm and most of my face, on the sidewalk and in a litter basket. I mean, they couldn't find enough of me, of unburned skin, for grafts." She laughed and touched her scalp. "I think they used the surgeon's rubber gloves on my head. I hurt a lot, and I have . . . seizures when I black out and can't remember anything.

I have phlebitis because I have to lie flat on my back in bed for days at a time. And on top of that I had people spraying seminal fluid up me every five minutes. But, Willis, I survive, don't I? You had an accident when you were a kid. So did I. So what? Every day I write in my *journal*, just to document this great life! It's *now* now. And if people spray seminal fluid at you, you spray 'em back in spades—get 'em like we did Basil Schrantz! If somebody kills you, kill 'em back *in spades*! You know what I mean. Just enough to scare 'em."

I nodded, trying to follow her reasoning.

"I'm not saying an eye for an eye here. I'm saying a leg, an arm, an internal organ, *and* an eye for an eye. But be *fair* about it. Have a little mercy."

She burped again.

"Whatever you say, Iris."

"Willis, God's telling me something . . . hold on. Hold *on*. She's sayin' to me that the guy's gonna show up *tonight*. Face him. Fight him. *Wake up*, Willis! I'm getting angry, I'm talkin' to *you*!"

"*Who* is God saying will walk out of my apartment alive?"

She patted my arm, suppressing another blast, puffing out her cheeks.

"Coke gives me gas," she said.

Later, after I'd met her yoga instructor and the crafts teacher and some other patients, I shook hands good-bye. Iris stood by my side as I waited for my taxi. She leaned very close, her ripped mouth panting, her loose eye rolling kindly in my direction.

To my horror, she began to cry. "You haven't really heard anything I've said," she whimpered. Nina appeared out of nowhere and began weeping too, standing on one foot and then the other. She reached out her arms to Iris, then tentatively embraced her. I put my arms around them both and joined in the tears.

"Iris," I sobbed. "I'm sorry."

We all cried, holding on, weaving back and forth.

"Here, Iris." I fished in my bag and gave her the extra key to my apartment, the one I'd forgotten to deliver to Terence at a high point in our romantic evening the night before. "Come anytime you need to talk," I said. I kissed her and pulled softly away from Nina. Nina stopped me, looked into my eyes, and gave my face a long, wet lick.

"Breathe deeply. Count backward from ten," she said.

"Good-bye," I said.

Just then a man in a white tunic came up. He had cultivated my least-favorite male hairstyle. He was balding slightly, but had grown his hair long—in a flowing Beatles "do." He looked like an aging George Harrison, but *mean*, with a caymanlike jaw that sprang open and shut with force.

"Iris. Nina," he crooned. "Time for Group."

They shrugged. Iris dried her eyes, winked, and showed me the key already hidden in her sleeve. She smiled at The Cayman. "Group sucks," she said sweetly. Nina was still crying. Iris waved and walked off with her, helping her along the path.

The Beatle-Cayman-Doctor looked at me from under his bangs. "I understand you're the SISTERHOOD reporter whom Iris contacted. It's *phenomenal*. I can't tell you, really, what this has done to the *rest* of us, who are *also* victims— in the sense that we were completely ignorant about what was going down here. This has been a *shock* to everybody. But we're grateful that it came to light, I can share *that* with you!"

I looked away. The guy was probably perfectly okay, but I was in no mood for shrinks. I searched the long drive in vain for a sign of my taxi. Then I checked out his name plate.

"Dr. Bush, I'm not a reporter. I'm an editor."

"And *I'm* not *just* Dr. Bush, I'm director of this institution.

Hey, I don't mean to overwhelm you—this is no *power* trip—but my position *does* give me a particular perspective on your *gamble.*"

I felt myself getting angry. *"What* gamble?"

"Well. The *obvious.* I mean, what kind of person trusts a completely disturbed voice out of *nowhere?"* He laughed, an unpleasant sound. "Let's face it: I *adore* our Iris, but she's at risk. I'll share with you that she is clearly not our most integrated personality. But you knew *that!"* He laughed his horrid laugh again.

"The letter made sense to *me.* And it proved to be true. So what's your *point?"* I glared at him.

"Yeees," he crooned. He pushed his bangs back and touched his wispy mane self-consciously. "You were very *lucky.* This could have all backfired in your face, sweetheart— *what* is your name?"

"Digby. Willis Digby."

"Miss Digby. Iris is so delusional—oh, God, how does one make it real to the uninitiated? And something tells me *you've* never been in therapy! Well, let's start here—Iris is so *delusional* that it's almost impossible for her to separate her invented realities from what is actually happening to her. I'll share with you that it's a limited-progress case. I'm sure she's told you about her life. The mother was psychotic, suicidal, killed herself and tried to kill her little girl, Iris. She opened a gas valve, then took a cigarette lighter to it. Forced little Iris to stand next to her, hold the flame."

"Bull*shit!"* I yelled. A few people looked over. "Iris's mother was beautiful, a beautiful, kind woman with auburn hair in a goddamn French twist—an ice-cream truck had a generator explosion and it blew her up."

"Oh, *sure!"* He laughed his ghastly snort-laugh. "You liked that story?" He pushed his big bangs out of his eyes again, to give me his sincerest look. "It's one of many she tells herself, Miss Digby, to help herself cope with the incomprehensible and unending horror of her life. She had a *murderess* for a mother! And can you imagine living inside that *body*?" He clucked like a hen. "She tells stories; she invents love. Hasn't she told you that she thinks she's beautiful?" He smirked a little.

The cab finally poked into the drive. I waved it down. I was shaking. I picked up my bag and stared into his nasty little shrink's eyes.

"Iris," I said, "*is* beautiful. Personally, I find her one of the most beautiful women I have ever seen. I believe everything she says. I honor it." I pulled open the cab door, threw my bag inside, and looked back. "What do *you* honor?"

He smirked again and put on a "naughty-boy" look. "Oh-oh. I seem to have touched a nerve."

I got in and slammed the door shut. "If you're a *good* guy, I can't wait to see what they put behind bars. Thanks to *Iris*."

The cab shuddered off, with a spray of gravel. The good doctor stood smirking on the curb.

Fifteen

The train was late; the train was hot. At Grand Central I decided not to bother putting an appearance in at work at all; I'd go home. Whatever happened happened. I would call Terence and invite him over after the show. If he couldn't come, I'd stay there alone.

I found a bank of pay phones and actually located one that *worked*—next to a woman dressed like Chiquita Banana. She wore leopard skin toreador pants, a gold reflecting bolero, Carmen Miranda makeup, and a bunch of bright yellow plastic bananas on her head. She smiled over at me, and as she continued speaking into the phone, passed me a card that read:

MEXICALI MAMMA

She *dances*, tells you your fortune, (who will you marry? will you or others be rich or dead?) and *sings* the most big walloping hits from South of the Border!

Telephone (any hour) 111-5522

I smiled and nodded, pocketing the card. *She* smiled and nodded, shaking her bananas.

I got Terence at home.

"Listen, Willis," he said. "I've had it. You can't live like this anymore. *I* can't live like this—worrying about you all the time! The play gets out at ten twelve. I'll be showered and out of the dressing room and at your place by ten-thirty. Meet me there and we'll face this psycho together."

"I *can't*. I've been out of town and I'm at Grand Central. I'm not going in to work, it's already almost five. I'm going to grab something to eat and go home *now*. I'm *tired*."

"*Okay. Go home*, drop your stuff off, say hello to your walls, and then get out of there again. Go to a movie—come up here, sleep in my dressing room, *something*—till I get there. *Please*. Let me protect you from this."

A pause.

"Willis?"

I was thinking. I was experiencing reaffirmation (in the parlance of my age) about this guy: I was thinking, *he's a hero, Terence. He's a goddamn hero after all*. (The snag was, I had to rearrange my schedule to allow him to be one. But there it was.)

"Okay," I said meekly. "Okay. I'll just drop some things off and I'll go take in a movie somewhere. I'll meet you at my place at ten-thirty."

"*Sharp*."

"Sharp."

"And, Willis?"

"Yeah?"

"Don't worry about *anything*, I can handle this guy. Okay?"

"Okay, Terence. Thanks."

I hung up. I took the local home. When I got there, Whizzer opened the door and shook a gloved finger at me. He was the world's slowest talker. I waited for him to glance right and left, wet his lips, push back his visored hat, run a hand through his great white pompadour. Finally he was ready.

"Will . . . is. You're . . . late." He sighed and wet his lips again. "There's a . . . mag . . . a . . . zine . . . PA . . . PA . . . RA . . . ZZ . . . I . . . wait . . . ing . . . up . . ."

I couldn't wait for the gumball.

"Goddamnit!" I threw my bag down. Whizzer, who'd still been forming words, jumped. His gloved hand fluttered to his lips, as if to block the assembly line of slow-moving words.

I'd forgotten all about the interview Minnie had set up for me.

"Whizzer, *c'mon.* You know you're not supposed to let anyone upstairs without telling me first."

He started to gear up again. "Will . . . is?" He caressed his amazing white hair again and nodded several times, as if he'd begun receiving messages through a hidden earpiece.

"I . . . *told* . . . them . . . ab . . . so . . . lute . . . ly . . . *no,"* he began. Several eternities later, he'd managed to explain that Minnie had arrived in a cab from SIS with PA-PARAZZI in tow. She'd told Whizzer that I'd approved everything—he also made sure, he told me proudly, that he was shown an official press I.D. (*I . . . D . . .*)

"Will . . . is." A long pause. "Did . . . I . . . do . . . wrong?"

I sighed. "It's okay, Whizzer. It's not really your fault. I just don't feel like doing this today. Is Minnie still up there?"

He looked right and left, pushed back his visor, wet his lips.

"Wait," I cried, "she got mad and left, right? She told me to call her at the magazine, right? *Try* not to *talk,* Whizzer. Just nod yes or no."

He made a sound somewhere between a belch and a muted scream as he cut off the goose-stepping syllables.

Then he looked right and left, pushed back his visor, wet his lips, and nodded yes.

Sitting on the floor outside my apartment, collapsed next to a pyramid of cameras and lighting equipment, was a good-looking, very tired young man with a laminated PAPARAZZI press card clipped to his leather jacket. He was half-dozing, his long legs in jeans stretched out into the hall, his dark hair falling into his eyes.

I took a deep breath. "I'm sorry I'm late. I forgot about this interview."

He jumped so violently that he popped the lens cover off the camera he was holding in his hands—it went crazily rolling into the door. He shook his head and pulled himself up to a sitting position. "Christ!" he said. "Christ." Then he grinned up at me good-naturedly. "You really sent me. I was just nodding out a little here." He stood up and offered his hand.

"Perry Tate."

"Willis Digby—I'm sorry to have kept you waiting so long."

He grinned again. "Beats chasing Liza around Studio 54."

"It *does*? Sleeping in an apartment hallway? She must be *something*."

He laughed, then noticed me looking at his press card. "My writer went out for coffee. She got a little impatient. Oh, yeah, and your friend Minnie got pretty pissed off after an hour or so. She took off."

"We can manage without Minnie." I unlocked the door and he hoisted the cameras and the jumble of lenses and light meters over his shoulder, ducked his head at the door. I switched on the lights.

"Would you like some coffee or something?" I threw down my bag with an ominous *chunk*, remembering, too late, my Crafts Fair purchases. I pulled them out—the ashtray was broken, but the other stuff looked okay. I pulled out the tea cozy and the wire Empire State Building and took them out to the kitchen with me.

"I'm sorry," I said. "I wasn't listening. What did you say you wanted?"

"Well, maybe a Diet Pepsi—if you have it." He was kneeling near a window, unpacking his lighting equipment.

"Lemme check." I put the stuff down and opened the refrigerator. Amazingly, I had a diet soda of some sort and a cream soda for me.

"I'm really kind of relieved you're here," I called, opening the can. "I'm being harassed by this weird guy, a Peeping Tom who's gotten very aggressive lately."

"Dammit," I heard him curse softly as he dropped a piece of equipment. "Oh, yeah?" he called. "How does he get up high enough to see in the windows?"

I brought him the diet soda. "I think he stands on the sidewalk when he looks in here. You can see lights go on and off from down there. It turns out, though, that he can see *right into* my office at work—*he* works in some office building that's right across from SIS, or really close by." I peered out the window at Third Avenue below. It was starting to get dark.

"How do you know?" He drank some soda, pushed his hair back.

"The guy writes to me. He writes me these weird letters— God, you should see them!" I laughed, though I was shocked that I could make light of the whole thing. "I mean *weird*. Like he's some cross between J. D. Salinger and Norman Bates. A literary killer."

A phone in the kitchen rang. "That might be my writer," he said. "Oh, yeah, wait, I almost forgot. There was this letter for you at SIS—I thought I should bring it down to you." He pulled an envelope from his jacket pocket.

"There are *always* letters for me at SIS," I said. I took the envelope without looking and sprinted for the phone.

"Hello?"

"Willis, if you think just because you're getting some *media* attention right now, it's okay to make people wait for hours on end for you, you better think—"

"Minnie, I'm sorry. But you know, you really can't go ahead and schedule things for me without confirming them. Anyway, I'm busy right now, the photographer is here setting up, and the writer is coming over in a minute."

"What writer?"

"The *writer*, Minnie! They always travel in twos, photographer and writer."

I was slouched in the kitchen doorway, looking into the living room at Perry Tate. He stood up and faced me, a camera in front of his face. He turned the rings, focusing.

"Well, *this* guy didn't. He told me, *he* was the writer *and* the photographer. There wasn't any writer with him." She paused. "Anyway, they can always send a writer over *later*. I never knew this—Did you know this? There's a branch of PAPARAZZI *right across* from us. I could throw a stone out these windows and hit . . ."

I turned away from the living room, twisting the phone cord around my waist. I felt very calm, eerily calm.

"Minnie," I said softly. I heard my own voice talking, from far far away. *"Listen to me.* This is life and death, Minnie. Tell Page that PAPARAZZI is here, in my apartment. And then tell her that their offices are *right across from us* . . ."

"What? I can't hear you so well, Willis, you sound weird. What are you saying?" He was crossing the room, the camera still held up before his face, moving toward me. Somehow, without realizing what I was doing, I'd opened the letter—before I looked down at it, I knew what it would say. The famous handwriting. Three words.

"Willis? I'm going to hang up now. Betty Friedan just walked in. I *never* get over her presence! I'll call you back." She hung up.

I replaced the receiver. I turned and looked at The Watcher. The split second I turned, the flash went off and I was blinded. I heard him crossing the room swiftly.

I saw black and red circles before my eyes. I groped along the counter for a weapon, *any* weapon! A knife, a frying pan. My hand fell on something hard and cold.

When he grabbed me from behind, I turned and stabbed him in the neck with the Empire State Building. He cried out and grabbed at his throat. I saw blood. I came at him again, slashing with the spire, aiming for the jugular. I was sobbing. He made no sound, but his face was savage, canine. He grabbed for the Empire State Building and tried to twist it out of my grasp.

One of his fingernails ripped across my hand. I stabbed wildly with my weapon; he put his hands up against my attack. He fell backward against the kitchen door and I started kicking, in the general area of his crotch. I hit.

He fell to the floor, holding himself. I fell on top of him; I heard the wind go out of him. The Empire State Building cut through his shirt, his undershirt, the skin of his neck.

"You son of a bitch. You son of a bitch!" I gasped. "You wanna hurt me? You wanna hurt me?" I stabbed his arm. Blood welled up. "You bastard!" I was screaming so loud I couldn't hear myself. I stabbed his hands, held up against his chest and neck.

He grabbed at the Empire State Building. He fended it off, once, twice. "What are you doing?" he yelled. "What are you doing? You want to kill *me*? The way you killed Matthew Kallam?"

The name stood in the air. I hit him again, this time in

DEAR DIGBY

149

the chest. Then the name took hold. I pulled myself off him, pushing a hand, bloody, against the wall.

"Who the hell are you?" At last I heard my own voice—it sounded like an animal trying to speak. "WHO THE HELL ARE YOU?? How do you know these things about me?"

He sat up suddenly and hit the Empire State Building out of my hand. It skittered across the linoleum floor. He fell back, exhausted. "I'm Danny," he groaned. "I'm Danny."

"The name means nothing to me, fuckhead." I looked at the Empire State Building lying propped against the refrigerator. I began crawling toward it. I looked back. "You'll have to do better than that."

He touched his hand to his face and looked at it. He was covered with bloody cuts, and blood had welled up in the hollow of his neck. "Danny Hayburn," he said in a tight small voice. "I was in the tent the night you shot Matthew Kallam."

For one wild second I believed him. I believed that he was the ghost who'd been following, just a little bit behind me, since the night Matthew died. He was Justice—now he would stand up in armor made of flames and hold out the sword. I would be judged and released into Hell. I would be freed at last. Unequivocally damned.

Then I returned to myself. I rested my hand on the Empire State Building. He and I stared at each other. He looked like an actor in a horror movie; blood had run in rivulets down his face and neck and had soiled his collar and shirtfront. Abruptly he pulled himself up to a sitting position. I brandished my weapon like a switchblade. He eased back against the wall.

"You say you were in the tent. *What* tent are you talking about? Where? And what was your father's name?"

"The *tent*," he said in a surprised, vaguely hostile tone. "The tent in the countryside"—he looked at his bloody hands—"about . . . fifteen miles outside Carlisle, Pennsylvania. Where *my* father, Colonel Martin Hayburn, and *your* father"—he bowed sarcastically—"Colonel Homer Digby, went pheasant hunting." He rubbed at his eyes, unconsciously smearing blood around them. "At the time they were attending the War College." He bowed again. "The War College at Carlisle."

He looked at me, and again he took on the glow of Avenging Angel. But the blood around his eyes made his gaze diabolical. I relaxed my hold slightly on the Empire State Building, but I kept it up, between us. I tried hard to see the child in the tent, little Danny Hayburn, ten-year-old warrior, in his face, but I was too frightened to remember. I could only imagine.

My fury came back. "Let's say you *are* Danny Hayburn— why the fuck are you *doing* this to me?"

Just then the refrigerator came to life with a galvanized shudder. I jumped and so did he.

He leaned forward confidentially. I held my weapon up. "I'd like to help you," he said.

I started to laugh and then couldn't stop. "*Help* me???"

The phone started ringing. I made the mistake of glancing at it—and he was on top of me. He had the Empire State Building out of my hand before I knew what was happening. *This* time he lobbed it into the living room. I heard it hit the far wall and clatter away.

He jerked my arm half out of the socket. "Sit *still*."

The phone rang and rang. Eight times. We stared at each other, not moving. I thanked God I hadn't put my answering machine on—there must be somebody out there who would think it odd that I wasn't picking up at home. I thought of my conversation with Terence—*he* wouldn't call because he thought I was staring at a film somewhere—anyway (I glanced at the clock) it was seven. Too late for a call from him even if he'd thought to double-check my whereabouts. At seven he'd already be manuevering into position, physically and psychologically, for the raising of the eight o'clock curtain. He'd be limbering up, doing body and throat exercises, yoga; he'd be saying a troublesome line over and over, sipping lemon and honey, his concentration on the dialogue, his stage presence, intensifying second by second. Then when the curtain went up, no emergency of the outside world (short of nuclear war) could touch him till the play was over. *Still, if I can keep this guy at bay till the play's over*, I thought grimly, *Terence will handle him.*

A quick peripheral scan told me that there was nothing close by to pick up and bean him with. Up on the counter were knives, frying pans, a pizza cutter. I thought of the .38 in the bedroom drawer—it might as well have been in Brooklyn.

I looked into those strange eyes, rimmed with blood, flecked with gold, very clear yellow eyes. When I stared in his direction, they lit up like a jack-o'-lantern. *Talk*, I ordered myself. Talk to the maniac. I recalled a TV thriller where Farrah Fawcett or some other determined starlet soothed a psychotic killer who'd broken into her apartment by teaching him how to crochet. Could *I* do that?

"You're lucky." He leaned in close to me. "You didn't try to pick up that phone."

I tried to smile in a placating way. My mouth muscles weren't working very well. "So you're Danny, Colonel Hayburn's son."

I was trying to move my rump, a fraction of an inch at a time, closer to the counter. He raised a bloody hand.

"Don't. You see, I really *don't* want to hurt you, but I *will* if you insist on trying to get away. You're just going to have to *listen*. I have some things to say to you. I think they'll *help* you. So pay attention."

I relaxed. "Listen, Danny. I'm sure we can make some . . . agreement here."

The hazel eyes blinked.

"I'm willing to forget this whole thing: your getting in here, the letters, everything. If you'll just get up and go now, I won't even call the police."

Silence. I forced myself to smile at him.

"You're not badly hurt—just a few cuts on your face. I'm *sorry* about that, but you know, you . . . *scared* me. So if you'll just leave now . . ."

Long silence. Then he smiled.

"I want to take your picture." He started to get up, then looked at me. "Do you promise you'll stay here and not move?"

I smiled again. "Sure."

He steadied himself against the wall, then turned toward his pile of camera equipment. I lunged for the stove, the hanging pots and pans, the knife holder. I got halfway there. He grabbed me and spun me around, he plucked a dish towel from a hook and tied my wrists together, pushed me back down. He was making a growling sound.

"Don't *lie* to me," he said. "I told you before, I don't *want* to hurt you. *Why* do you have to push me like this?"

Then he put a hand very gently under my chin. "I can't believe I'm touching you. It's extraordinary to see you're real. Extraordinary." I watched the Avenging Angel return. "Don't try any of that shit again! I'm warning you."

I sat still while he gathered up a camera and light meter. I looked at my wrists, my hands held together as if they were applauding.

After he'd waved the meter all around me, the intercom box on the wall near the door came to life, crackling and popping. It was Whizzer.

"Hi . . . Will . . . is." He cleared his throat twice. "Hope . . . every . . . thing . . . is . . . hunk . . . y . . . dor . . . y . . . up . . . there." He sighed, cleared his throat again. Silence.

The Watcher glared at the wall, then pulled me to my

feet again. "You tell him everything is okay," he hissed.

I racked my brain, trying to think of a code that Whizzer could crack. The box crackled again. "If . . . you're . . . too . . . bus-y . . . to . . . pick . . . up . . . right . . . now . . ."

I pushed the TALK button awkwardly with my bound hands. "No, Whizzer," I said. "*No*, thanks for checking on me! That's great. You know how *security-conscious* I am, always watching everything like a hawk—so I'm *grateful*, Whizzer."

There was a large foghornlike blast, and I realized that Whizzer had just blown his nose.

"Par . . . don . . . me . . . Al . . . ler . . . gies . . . You . . . know . . . Miss . . . us . . . Wall . . . en . . . stein's . . . cat . . ."

He sneezed loudly; the intercom box shook. He apologized, interminably.

I hit the TALK button again.

"Whizzer, if you could just *see* me now, you'd see that everything's . . ."

The Watcher crooked his elbow under my chin and pulled my head back. He looked down into my face.

"Tell him you're *fine*, *not* to come up. Do it *now*. Then say *good-bye*," he whispered. He let me go roughly, and I staggered forward.

"Whizzer," I croaked, "I'm fine. Don't bother coming up! Good-*bye!*"

"O . . . kay, Will . . . is. Nice . . . talk . . . ing . . . to . . . ya. When . . . ev . . . er . . . I . . . think . . . about . . . you . . . bein' . . . in . . . PA . . . PA . . . RAZZ . . . I . . . I . . . get . . . the . . . chills."

"Bye, Whizzer." I was nearly crying.

He took my picture. In fact, he took several pictures of me, sitting on the kitchen floor, my back against the refrigerator, my hands bound.

"Put a little *expression* in your face, Willis," he said at one point.

"I have some *great* shots of you that I took with a telephoto lens—from my office roof. You can see the goose bumps on your skin."

"How neat."

He looked hurt. The blood on his face had congealed into a dark webbing.

He reached into a camera bag and pulled out an envelope. "Look," he said.

I rubbed my eyes with my bound hands and looked. It *was* an extraordinary photograph. A black-and-white eight by ten. It was a picture of me, in my tux and rabbit ears, but it wasn't amusing. It had been taken with a telephoto lens through plate glass, but the texture was coarse and clear. I was standing in an office window, high over Manhattan, looking down. The background was flat, except for the frozen metallic flash of a window or two. I looked like a cabaret artiste who'd just taken off her makeup, my eyes and mouth wiped clean of expression in the flat light. My face wiped away to a bald suffering slate.

"I call it 'Letters to the Editor.' " He gave me a meaningful look.

"Look at *these*." He fanned out twenty or so matte photographs. Me running in the rain down Lex, my arm thrown up in a taxi *Sieg Heil*; me falling asleep in my collar on the IRT; eating Szechwan with Page, my chopsticks poised above a plate of noodles; me in a phone booth, laughing hard.

"Why do you take these pictures of me?"

"I document *everything*. I videotaped my goldfish giving birth last week—I actually have a tape of my budgie having a seizure." He snorted at his own humor. Then he looked away from me, across the living room, and the big cat's eyes in his gory face lit up. "To me, you're a living document."

He got me on my feet and led me into a room I call my

study, a nook off the living room. Only a Japanese screen makes it private.

It was dark; there was a little light from the window—city reflections. I hunkered down on the Moroccan rug. Not far from me a brass letter opener gleamed on the desk top.

He took some things out of a leather bag, muttering to himself: an Orange Crush bottle, a lantern, and a .22 rifle in a case.

He yanked out four cushions from the sofa, set them in a circle, and put the bottle in the middle of the circle. He lit the lantern; it took him a while to get the wick going, then it flared and shadows leaped onto the walls, eerie as cave drawings.

He gave me his Halloween smile. "Remind you of anything?" I smiled and nodded. I was trying to cover my desperate work on the dish-towel tourniquet around my wrists. I was surreptitiously sawing it against the radiator frame.

He walked over. He took my arm and dragged me over a few feet.

"Don't *try it!*" He got up and put the letter opener in a drawer, turned and winked at me. "I've got eyes in the back of my head."

"Danny," I said, "listen to me. . . ."

He bent down and kissed my bound hands. "I'm so sorry about this. I didn't want to have to tie you up. I wanted us to have *rapport.*" Then he took a bandanna from his jeans pocket and tied my ankles together.

I stared at the dried blood that clotted his eyelashes. They fluttered, giving him a made-up, geishalike look. He lowered his lashes and talked about how he'd wanted us to be friends. Then I'd printed his letter and he saw he'd have to try another approach. It was time to change the story. He looked over his shoulder at the tableau set up in the middle of the room. "I'm *ending* this story."

"Just let me go, really, it's better!" I tried to get him to look at me. "Whatever this is all about—we can meet for a drink sometime and talk about it. But right now . . ."

"I've watched you so closely." He raised his voice slightly, still looking at me. "I know everything about you. Your taste in books"—he swept his hand around to include my library—"is exactly what I expected." He moved to a bookshelf and touched the worn spine of a book reverently. *"To the Lighthouse"* he intoned. "God. Mrs. fucking *Ramsay."*

He caressed the book. "One of the most moving characters in literature," he whispered. "And how does she *die?"*

"In a *bracket,"* I answered without thinking. That peculiarly Woolfian demise had always angered and hurt me, too.

He nodded and shook his head at me again, laughing at our twinned, tragic sense. Then he picked up the .22. I flattened against the wall. He pulled a box from his jacket pocket, opened the rifle case, and took out the gun. He shook the bullets out of the box and loaded the magazine from the front. Then he put on the safety.

"I'm not going to hurt you," he said. "I'm just going to *talk* a little." He pointed the gun at a framed photo of Holly Partz on the wall. "I never liked that woman," he said. Then he spun around and pointed the gun at me. I slid, scraping my vertebrae, down the wall.

"Listen!" Now he looked down the barrel at the sofa cushions.

I pulled myself back up and paid attention.

"Once upon a time there were three boys who loved to hunt together. We used to hunt by the river with BB guns and .22s. We had dugouts in the high grass. We were like brothers—and Matthew was the oldest. Matthew was powerful. He knew how to rule. He beat up every other kid who refused to acknowledge his supremacy—but I was one of the ones who acknowledged it. I was a little younger than him. I thought being mean was his privilege. He liked having Stevie, the third member of our group, around because he was young and easy to boss around and his father owned a lot of the land we hunted on. He was our mascot.

"Then, Willis"—he knelt next to me, knightlike, the rifle planted like a standard—"one day *you* came *with* us. Our dads told us we had to put up with you coming. They were humoring your dad, they said. We hated you—a trespasser in our private kingdom. You came marching out with your red hunting cap and field boots, very serious. Skinny and tall for your age. We were all laughing at you behind your back. Then the dogs started pointing and you began to shoot—good God!" He shook his head; the yellow eyes blinked in their blood mask. "You could nail anything, moving or not. Matthew was furious. He whispered to me, 'She's asking for it.' He got madder and madder. When he missed shots, he kicked the dogs. You didn't seem to notice him. Neither did your dad, except once he said, 'Kurt, your boy Matt shoots a little wild—he oughta go out with my Willis one day. She could give him a few pointers.' "

I laughed out loud. I hadn't heard anything like that.

"Before we went in the tent for the night, your dad took me aside. 'Would you watch out for my daughter?' he said. 'She can take care of herself, but she might need a friend.' "

"He said that to you?"

He smiled. "He did. I was a little afraid of him, but I felt flattered. I said sure, I'd watch out for you.

"Then, in the tent, I could see you getting scared. You knew Matthew a little from school, and you tried to kid around with him. But it didn't work because Matthew was feeling like you had stolen something from him. And you had."

"I hadn't stolen anything. It belonged to me too."

He got up. He nudged the Orange Crush bottle with the toe of his Frye boot. The lantern light rocketed around, pinned to the bottle, and for one ghastly second the four lumps around the bottle looked lifelike: slouched figures, kids.

He stood facing the window, remembering. "I didn't understand right away what Matthew had in mind with Spin the Bottle—when I saw he was *serious*, it was too late, you were already rolling over each other on the floor. I saw you pick up the .22—and then I knew what was going to happen."

I found my voice. "Why didn't you try to help me before that?"

He poked at one of the cushions with the barrel of the .22. "I was afraid. And I stayed afraid, all the days afterward—I never gave anyone my account of what happened."

He stabbed at the cushions with the .22. "And then it all moved so fast. They hushed it up—they had an autopsy but no inquest. Even the coroner, I guess, didn't want criminal charges brought. They all said it was an accident."

"It *was* an accident."

"No," he said, "it wasn't. I was there in the tent. They just hushed it up, and pretty soon everyone had forgotten or moved on. I was the only one who remembered—and I remembered everything. I heard you went off to college, became an antiwar activist, broke with your dad. Then I heard you worked for a famous magazine in Manhattan. I heard gossip about all these things—by now I was a professional photographer for a magazine that made its *name* on gossip.

"One day I was walking back to my offices from lunch and I heard someone say, 'I'm Willis Digby,' and there you were among the mail sacks. And I knew immediately that you were hurt by something and I knew what it was. I knew it was that childhood death. I *did* follow you. I *did* watch you, yes, because I wanted to see who you'd become. Mostly, I liked you." He laughed. "I mean, you could have been a *jerk*."

"It wasn't necessary to spy on me." I waggled my feet up and down to keep the circulation going. "Why didn't you just call me up and introduce yourself? Why did you try to scare me?"

He laid the .22 on the floor beside him.

"It wasn't my intention to scare you." He touched my knee, then quickly pulled his hand back. "I told you, I thought that writing you letters was a gentle way to enter your life. I thought you'd begin to like me, to answer my letters. We'd get to be friends. I wouldn't just crash through the door and say what I had to say."

"Oh, yeah, perish *that* thought."

He bowed his head. "I saw your father right before he left for Vietnam. The *day* before."

I felt a chill.

"Yeah." His face tightened and he ran a finger along the gun barrel. "I went to see him. My life was really screwed up right then. I was depressed and flunking out of school and I wanted his advice. I wanted to enlist. I thought I'd try and be a military man like my dad."

"Oh, yeah? Did he give you the rah-rah 'you too can be a second lieutenant' rap?"

"No. As a matter of fact, he didn't. He remembered me right away, and he remembered that my father had died a few years before. We went out and had a drink. Well, we had a *few* drinks. I told him that I was ready to go to Nam. I didn't give a shit if I died. He grabbed my arm. *'Don't enlist,'* he said. 'Do anything but enlist, and if they try to draft you, run. Go to Canada, go to Mexico. Don't go over there and get killed in that stupid, wasteful, pointless war.' "

There was a long silence. "You're quoting *my* father?" The .22 was lying maybe two feet away from me now, but I couldn't seem to move. I was trying to imagine the conversation: my father and this skittish young madman.

"He said he was going over there to assist with the withdrawal process, and he had to appear publicly to support it. He asked me if I ever saw you, and I lied and said I did. In fact, I may have even made it sound like we were *close.*" He glanced over at me. "He told me to tell you something. He said to tell you that you were right about the war. And that he couldn't admit it to your face. But he was on your side."

"I saw him too, just before you did. Why wouldn't he have told *me* all this? He was *Patton* when *I* was there."

"Maybe he *tried.* He told me that when he saw you, he asked you for *mercy.*" He put his head down and began to cry. "I should have found you and told you this long ago. Especially after I heard he went over there and died." His whole face dissolved in tears.

I felt clearer-headed suddenly. "Untie my hands and feet," I demanded. He looked up. He loosened the bandanna around my ankles.

"Wait. There's one last thing." He got up with the rifle in one hand and kicked the bottle into motion again. Then he kicked one cushion on top of the another. He was shaking visibly—he held his left arm across his stomach and bent over slightly, as if he'd been socked in the solar plexus. Suddenly he straightened up and pointed with the .22.

"You were like *this,* you and Matthew." His voice broke. "Get it? Do you get it?" He looked frantically at me for affirmation. I nodded. "On top of each other and you were *rolling.* It was absolutely quiet and you rolled over and over. First I'd see his face, then your face. You looked so *desperate,* God!" He turned his head away. I thought he was going to weep, but he caught himself. He pointed with the rifle again. "Each time your face flashed by, I thought you were looking at me, crying, *'Help me, why don't you help me?'* " He put his head down, controlled himself. "I couldn't get my *aim,*" he cried. "It was so hard to get a clear shot, and then when I got it"—he lined up, sighting the two cushions—"I heard your .22 go off a fraction of a second before *I* shot—then *I* shot Matthew Kallam dead in the left side. Then *your* gun went off one last time, into the air, as it fell free. Everybody was screaming; right after that, everybody was confused."

Then he pulled the trigger; the top cushion blew apart, lifting right off the bottom one; the side split open, stuffing pouring out. The windows shook in their frames for a while; the sound echoed through the apartment and out into the hall. He stepped back, the smoking gun at his side, and knelt before me. He held his palms out flat, *voilà*. He was still shaking.

I tried to speak. "*You* killed Matthew Kallam? You never told anybody?"

"Only one other person. I told your father that night."

I felt dizzy. "What did my father say?"

The phone started ringing again. My neighbors were calling to ask what the noise was. I made no move to answer.

"First I thought he was going to strike me. Then he sat there and he put his head in his hands. He told me to tell you but *carefully*. He said not to spring it on you all at once. And he told me to go to the authorities. But I couldn't do that. All these years I was trying to get to *this*. To do what he asked me to do outside the tent that night: to watch out for you."

I stared at him. I thought I heard the apartment door open, but I was too far gone to pay attention.

"One spring I went up to Carlisle," he said. "I used my press credentials, and I gained access to the autopsy file photographs at the morgue. I managed to get a copy of one, don't ask me how." He produced a large manila envelope from his prop bag. A black-and-white 8 by 10. Matthew. A few hours after death, lying on a steel table, his arms folded calmly across his chest. Just before the electric saw, I thought, and held on. He looked so small and forthright, his eyes wide open, looking at me. Absolved of all his eleven-year-old terrors: a little kid. He had a broad forehead and wide-set eyes, but they were the door to an unformed face. He still had baby fat on his cheeks and arms. The only adult thing about him was the silver dog tags around his neck. His father's, from some war or other. Blood had congealed on his collarbone, where a bullet had grazed him. Under his left armpit there was a much larger, black wound; blood still seeped from it. "Upper thoracic, entry from the left," Danny pointed out, over my shoulder. "You don't need a degree in ballistics to read that story." I looked for a long time at the perfect concentration of his childish features, the disappeared light in his eyes. After twenty-three years I wept for him, someone's little boy, lost forever.

"What I need is someone to forgive me," Danny said. He looked at me and reached out for the photograph. Then we both jumped as the Japanese screen fell over with a crash. Iris Moss stood in the doorway framed by light. Her rolling eye caught a beam like clear glass marble, and her strange mouth opened and closed, hissing. She was talking to herself. On her head was the Afro wig and on her body was a gold Lurex running suit with spangled epaulets. She held the .38 at an odd angle in her prosthetic hand.

"Don't move!" ("molve," in fact) she cried to Danny, who reeled to his feet in shock and horror, turning to run. I watched Iris take a cop-show stance, legs apart, brace-hand. I was screaming at her to stop, but she didn't hear; she took aim and shot—the bullet hit a brass music stand my mother had given me, then ricocheted, whining, struck The Watcher plumb in the left buttock.

Sixteen

"I'm convinced now that Death looks like Crazy Eddie,"
Page said. We were jogging down the old West Side Highway. The sun was setting over New Jersey. We had started
at 59th Street and were running to the West Village. We
were about at 34th Street.

It was two days after my showdown with The Watcher. I
was just starting to feel normal again. I was glad Page had
suggested this jog. She was trying to be discreet, but dis-
cretion was hardly her natural style. She kept shooting odd
interrogatory looks at me as she chatted breathlessly. Because she was talking so much, each mile seemed to get a
little harder for her; every so often she had an attack of little
hiccups.

"As I was drifting off to sleep the other night, he was on
the tube, casually sledge-hammering a nineteen-inch color
TV. I had a dream that he was an archangel and his job was
to sneak to the room where the person was dying with
dignity and smash the TV screen. Then God would appear
on the cracked screen and thank Eddie, as if he were an

Oscar emcee, and then God would give a commercial for heaven. I don't remember much about heaven, but there was a Tiki village colored-water fountain and mariachi bands." She pushed her sweatband back on her head and grimaced.

"Who did God look like?" I asked.

"God looked exactly like Margaret Rutherford."

"I don't think Death looks like Crazy Eddie, and I don't think you see a light that asks you questions about your conduct. I think it's all chocolate pudding after they pull the plug," I said.

"You came pretty close to the Big Dessert the other night." She glanced sideways at me. She'd finally brought the subject up. She'd called the cops after Minnie had *insinuated* a form of my message about PAPARAZZI to her. But when she'd arrived at my apartment building, there was a police cordon outside in the street, and they wouldn't let her in. I'd spent the whole following day with police and Brookheart people—this was her first chance to catch up, beyond what had been on the news and a brief phone conversation, wherein I'd given her The Watcher's background.

"When I saw Iris with the .38, I thought we'd all bought it," I said. We slowed down a little, settling into a "long talk" stride.

"But then, after the smoke cleared, I checked Danny's wound—his name is Danny Hayburn—and it looked superficial. I got him some bandages and tried to clean it out. He was kind of in shock and moaning a lot. Iris was just standing there, holding the gun with both hands, looking *amazed*. After I stopped the bleeding, I went over to her, and she told me she had only meant to fire a *warning* shot, like the cops do—she said she was trying (for some reason) to hit the *stereo*. I took the gun and emptied the bullets out—and then all hell broke lose. Whizzer came crashing in, then the police, then Lupé with about fifteen Witches."

Page slowed down again and pushed at her sweaty headband.

"What about Terence? Where was *he*?"

"All night long I'd been waiting for him to throw open the door and beat his chest and swing in on a vine. Right after the play was over, he was due at my apartment, which was, ironically, right around the time Iris *did* arrive."

"So what happened?"

"What happened? What happened was that he *drove* the play, he told me, about a hundred and fifty miles per hour. He cut the last act short, so short the other actors were left without lines in place. They were *furious*. There was murmuring in the audience, he said, even a boo or two. He raced off the stage at three minutes after ten—he'd taken *nine minutes* off the time. He put his head in the sink to get the makeup off—he wasn't even going to shower—grabbed his bag and hit the dressing room door. There was a man standing there, blocking it, he said, very distinguished-looking, foreign. 'Excuse me,' he said to the guy, 'I'm trying to get somewhere *fast*!' The guy said, 'Yes, I noticed. I've never seen much frantic energy onstage before, you were *obsessed*!' "

Page looked at me. "Okay. Who *was* he?"

"Miloslav Kuchera, the famous Czech film director." Page stopped running. I stopped running and we faced each other.

"He told Terence he had only an hour or two before flying back to Prague. He had never seen such a performance, and he wanted to talk to Terence, over drinks, *just for a moment*, about the possibility of Terence appearing in his new film."

Page began to laugh. I began to laugh. We leaned against each other, laughing.

"What time did he finally get there?"

"Midnight."

"Jesus." She hiccuped, out of control.

"Yeah." We started jogging again. "I was so *ready* for him to walk through that door, I was going to let him have it. Iris was still with me. The cops decided to let her stay, in my guardianship, till the Brookheart personnel got there, which was much later. They took Danny with them, limping and weeping—Whizzer left, the Witches left, Iris and I were having a beer. So Terence walks in, saying, 'What's happening?' "

Page hooted. "Did you get out the .38 again?"

I looked at her. "No. No, I didn't. You know, I *was* ready to kill him, but when I saw his face, I felt terrible for him. He was *devastated*. He felt he'd failed me miserably—"

"Well, Christ, Digby, he *had*."

"He sat down on the couch and started to cry."

"Jesus, Digby! I told you—never trust a guy who cries—they're *sadists* to a man."

"Yeah, I know. But I felt different about everything at that point. I mean, you have to remember I'd just had my whole life story rewritten that night. Page, I couldn't help thinking—how much did I care if he wasn't perfect? He told me that he refused to have a drink with Kuchera, but invited him to talk on the cab ride down to my apartment. When they couldn't find a cab in the after-theater crush, they hopped on the subway. And it got stuck between stations. Terence said Kuchera couldn't *believe* him. Terence was beating on the subway walls and pacing. Kuchera paced along with him—he kept repeating, "Ob-*sessed*. You are ob-*sessed!*"

"And you believed this story?"

"I don't know. Like I said, it was a bizarre night. Where was it written anyway that he had to *save* me? In what fairy tale? And Jesus—all my *life*, I realized, I'd been waiting for some man to *save* me! I couldn't believe it, but there it was. Well, I saved myself—or rather, Iris saved me—from Danny, who was *also* trying to save me. Wasn't he? Terence just didn't get there in time to save me from the *other* savers.

DEAR DIGBY

167

My God, I felt so good—I could *forgive* Terence, I could show him a little mercy. He *was* a hero, in his own weird way. Like everybody else that night. Do you know how strange I felt, standing there in my living room, watching Terence sob and Iris try to do her best to comfort him?"

"Yeah?"

"She asked him for a recent photograph, she brought him a handkerchief, she cut out a piece of his hair—a big piece— to put in her 'fan' scrapbook. Then the three of us sat there, Terence crying, me dozing, Iris mumbling to herself—holding hands for a while. It was very peaceful."

Page hiccuped again.

"After a while the Brookheart staff people arrived and picked up Iris, and then Terence and I sat there on the couch till dawn, holding hands and staring, like the last two people left on earth."

Page stopped running suddenly and crossed zigzaggedly over the highway line and sat down on the curb. The cars whizzed by below us, shaking the rickety foundation. "My heart is fluttering weirdly," she said.

I sat down next to her. I put two fingers on her wrist. "I can't get a pulse."

"It's okay. I don't think I have one. I've never been able to find it."

"Put your head between your legs," I said. She sat with her head between her herringbone leg warmers, her lovely red-brown hair falling onto her running shoes. "I'm okay," she said in a muffled voice. "I just don't want to die alone."

"*What?*"

There was a stifled sigh. "I'm *fine*. I've been thinking about the future. I don't have kids and I won't have kids—I doubt if I'll ever marry and all that's the way I want it. I just don't want to die all by myself."

She pulled her head up and looked at me. Her eyes were

bright brown. "Would you promise, Digby, to sit by my bedside when I'm dying?"

I took her hand in mine. "Page. What are you talking about? Why do I think that this has got something to do with Dresden Bostec?"

Dresden Bostec was a very young eighty-two. She visited the SIS office regularly with terrible-tasting home-baked pies and peckish moral support. Her older sister had been a suffragette, and she loved to talk about the Cause. She wore a coolie hat and smoked Camels. ("Hi, kids, I'm here to take the *suffer* out of *suffragette!*")

Once when she was in her seventies, Dresden Bostec had been hospitalized and told that she was dying. "And I thought I *was*, honey," she'd holler at anybody who was listening. She was lying in a bed alone in a hospital room, watching her life go by on the ceiling, and she pulled herself up and buzzed for a nurse. When the nurse came, she asked to hold her hand while she died, because, as she said, "there appears to be nobody else right now." The nurse took her hand and sat for a while. Dresden felt life draining from her and held tight. Then the nurse looked at her watch, told Dresden she had coffee break at six thirty. Dresden pulled her hand away and hoisted herself up. She peered at the nurse's watch; it said ten minutes after six. "I've decided not to die yet," she told the nurse. "I was too pissed off," she would confide later to her listeners. "Honey, I absolutely refused to croak just in time for her Sanka!"

Dresden lived on, but the deathbed scene did tend to stay with one. To have to grope hopelessly for a comforting hand at the end of the escalator was too cruel.

Page shrugged at me. "I'd ask Dresden, but she might be busy baking something that day." She sighed. "Or *worse*, she might *bring* me one of her pies in the hospital! I'm okay now," she said a little sheepishly. "This body is made of tensile steel."

I took her hand.

"I will write you a letter," I said. "A formal commitment signed, sealed, delivered. Saying that I will be by your side to take your hand on that sorry day."

She made a face at me, but she didn't take her hand away. "Thanks, Digby."

"Unless, dear pal," I said, "I've gone on *ahead*."

Seventeen

Dear Iris,

I know what you mean. I suppose it was inevitable, though, that Danny was sent to Brookheart for psychiatric observation. I think it's kind of encouraging that you're taking Classical Ballroom Dancing and Low Impact Aerobics together. And I'm positive that he is not the one who's smearing the Balm on the sanitary napkins. That sounds more like Dr. Bush.

As for me—well, ever since That Night, I've fallen asleep early in the evening and slept dreamlessly for ten, eleven, sometimes twelve hours. It's as if I'd satisfied my nightmare quota for the next thirty years. I get to sleep easy—no debts, no terrors. No more dreams of guns or babies. I still talk to Lily, but that's different. It's like you talking to God—she guides me.

Yes, Terence is still around and I've conveyed to him your desire for another photograph. And yes, I did notice that he looked at you with "stars in his eyes." Who wouldn't? He is being very solicitous to me too—he is still thankful that I am alive (as opposed to being, say, Republican), and therefore we are getting along well. He is feeling better himself. Have you ever noticed that physical threats to the loved one always quicken ardor? I think it's because there is a stand-in for one's own desire to maim or kill the loved one, thereby clearing the stage for protestations of devotion. I refer to the state that Terence and I are presently in as NYD, Not Yet Divorced. I prefer that description to, say, "desperately in love" or "inseparable" or "terminally gaga." If we can stay NYD for maybe two or three more years, I'll register my china pattern at Bloomingdale's. We are, in fact, living together and even discussing the act of procreation together, since that *is* what the Holy Father says sex is for. Oh, well, I can't fool you. Maybe we will stay together. Maybe we will have a kid one day. "Climb Mount Fuji, but slowly, slowly!"

And there's more news on the SIS front. Minnie W-W-G has changed her name to Solange. Just *one* name. No more hyphens, no more abbreviates. Just plain old Solange. The reason she changed her name is because she just broke off her engagement with a recalcitrant hyphenate.

Other SIS news: Bob Hargill so far has *not* sued me—in light of my now-somewhat-justified reasons for carrying a .38—but he has held a press conference, in which he accused me and W.I.T.C.H. of "urban terrorism." He has correctly identified W.I.T.C.H.'s intent as "invasion of privacy" and asked the city to "deal harshly" with any further such invasions. He has asked me for a public apology, which I intend to give him in a press conference of my own. W.I.T.C.H. has kindly engaged the services of a "hair reconstructionist," who will appear with me at the press conference and offer timely information to Bob (with visual aids) on his personal cosmetic (read Dome Shag) problem.

Needless to say, I have been inundated with letters, running about sixty-forty pro and con my new column. Holly has given me the okay to continue, at least for now. I finally met Dino Pedrelli, who showed up to shake my hand the other day—and to offer his services as a bodyguard. Since he's about four eleven with bifocals, I didn't leap at the opportunity—though he did point out to me that he owns a huge silver whistle that he uses to rout muggers, as well as to attract the attention of headwaiters, cabdrivers, and as he puts it, "people who are ignoring" him.

Yes, I was subpoenaed to testify in the Brookheart hearings, as expected. We'll probably be on the stand together. What they keep asking me is what made me answer your letter in the first place. Why wouldn't I? Everyone who writes to me expects to have an answer. Are we not supposed to answer people who say outrageous, outspoken things? No, we're not, we're supposed to all sound alike, all write alike, all make love alike. I promise not to preach—but what do you think about wearing matching plaid bloomers and gilt wedgies to court? *Women's Wear Daily* might be there, you never know.

As I said in response to a rather harshly worded inquiry of Page's yesterday: Yes, I probably will always talk like an asshole, thereby pissing people off, and that's just what makes this country great, isn't it?

One certainty: no more guns in my life, ever. In fact, I intend to do all I can to defeat that legalized vigilante lobby, the National Rifle Association. Those jerks should be lined up and shot!

No, I will never leave SIS; I love it. And I may never

leave Terence, since one great consolation in being involved with an actor is that the odds of his being in Madagascar on Monday are so much greater than in the average relationship.

I will be up to see you on Friday. I'll bring some more textbook Delusions and you can keep springing them on Bush. So far he's missed Sock Fetish, trichotillomania, and cyclothymia.

Terence and I (on the nights I'm not catching up on my sleep) have had a few forays into the glittering potholes of Manhattan night life. So far, though, I cannot (unlike the swallows) go back to Capistrano.

Write again soon,
WJD

P.S. Dear Iris,

The above is *not* the letter I meant to write. I wanted to write you a letter that explained my feelings for you—how I love you and how grateful I am to you.

It was a foggy day in New York City yesterday and I took a long walk. I love it when the edges of this sharp, clear city blur a little, when fog washes over the buildings like a white wave, when people emerge from the subways like phantoms. I walked along the East River—you couldn't see across it, which was nice. I felt safe, in a cocoon, carefully bandaged. I was afraid to take a deep breath, the way people with broken ribs are afraid to. Two people who are dead, gravely wounded by me, forgave me. They reached across time, touched me through time. At last I can bury my father, I can bless him as he has blessed me, and let him go, his daughter. I can bury Matthew Kallam, who all these years I thought I'd killed, whose ghost was as much a part of me as the blood in my veins. There's no particular comfort in knowing it wasn't *my* bullet that stopped his heart, because at that time I hated him and wanted him to die, *more* than Danny, but there's solace in seeing now how all our feelings in that tent that night were an accident, and how guns are designed to make the gunner feel nothing. Now I can feel something for that dead boy and for that little girl in hunting clothes, who sat beside his body, rocking back and forth in total silence as the fathers rushed in and the doctor . . . who said nothing about that night for twenty some years. *Mercy*, for us, and for Danny, mercy. Mercy for the little ghost who slipped from my womb, Lily, whom I still talk to —perhaps wrongly. Because that being was not Lily, it was a dreamer, a wanderer, not meant to quicken and be born. Mercy took her back into her great implausible ocean, where we all began, untouched. Well, another great thing about fog is that it's easier to walk around and cry in it. In fact, you can wail in it and who knows the difference.

My mother called and told me that she's going back to Carmel, where she's merely known as a bad painter and not the mother of a freak. Okay, okay. She *didn't* say that. What she said was, "I love you, honey, but you're just a little too weird for me." Which is fine because I know how she feels. I think I always knew I was a little too weird for her. I have been too weird for myself at times, but you've helped me shake hands with my strangeness.

I hope that this doesn't offend you but it does cheer me to know that you and Danny are in the same place. I think of you (forgive me) as a kind of late-life marriage, both injured (as *you* said) beyond repair, but kind, *kind* to each other.

I think of you as one of Van Gogh's "Irises," painted

at the end, in a so-called laughing academy—painted
among madmen, the gnarled, royal faces of the flowers,
and one white, one pure white.
   Dear one. I will visit soon.

Love,

Fog

Eighteen

Special to the New York Mirror— The State District Attorney's office suffered a setback in its upcoming patient abuse case against employees of the Brookheart State Hospital when a key prosecution witness, Ms. Iris Moss, thirty-five, a Brookheart resident for nineteen years, died earlier, today.

Ms. Moss was a victim of congestive heart failure, believed to have been caused by a pulmonary embolism, and succumbed at 6:00 A.M. EST in the intensive care unit of St. Philomena's Hospital, Badger Falls, New York.

Ms. Moss, who sustained second- and third-degree burns over 80 percent of her body as a childhood survivor of a fire that killed her mother, lived with dramatic physical and mental impairment as a result of burn trauma.

Throughout her life, she underwent regular extensive skin grafts (including painful scalp grafts, which never entirely healed). Her right hand and forearm were amputated, and she developed secondary pathologic conditions that included speech, neurologic and vision disorders, seizures, renal dysfunction, and chronic respiratory disease. She was also plagued by phlebitis (caused by periods of inactivity), and there is speculation, prior to the coroner's report, that a phlebitis attack precipitated the fatal embolism.

Despite her physical disorders, Ms. Moss was an active, outspoken member of the Brookheart community, President of the Patient's Rights Committee, member of the hospital's patient-staff liaison committee, President of the Brookheart David Letterman Fan Club, and chapter member of the Let's Stop Mr. Rogers Now Society.

She was an avid letter writer and it was her correspondence with a SISTERHOOD magazine editor that provided grounds for initial inquiry into staff conduct at Brookheart.

Ms. Moss, who was hospitalized in her early teens at Brookheart for minor personality disorders related to her various neurologic complaints, managed to overcome physical and mental adversities with an aggressively positive self-image. Attorneys in the D.A.'s office described her as "articulate, stubborn, opinionated, profoundly energetic."

The Brookheart hearings, scheduled for next week, will gain notoriety from prosecution plans to put several members of the Brookheart patient population on the witness stand. Ms. Moss's was to have been the central testimony in the hearings.

Funeral arrangements for Ms. Moss have not yet been set. There are no survivors.

I got the call about four A.M.—Iris had put me down as a relative on an "in case of emergency" form, and the head nurse told me I could enter the I.C.U. if I made it in time. I tried, but I didn't. Though Terence and I staggered out of bed and into our clothes and hit the thruway in record time, they'd taken her body away and Brookheart officials had signed for everything by the time we got to the hospital. I leaned against a pillar just outside the I.C.U. doors, like flotsam washed up by a great murderous swell. After hours in the dark warm car, the bright lights and antiseptic white walls hurt my eyes. Terence took my arm and tried to lead me away, but just then a brown-skinned busy little nurse bustled through the swinging doors of the I.C.U.

Carol Muske-Dukes

178

She took off her mask. "Are you Willis Digby?" she asked. Her eyes looked like she'd had enough for one night. She handed me a piece of paper. "She couldn't speak at the end, but she wrote most of these things down—I finished the rest using the letter chart." She gave me a professional smile. "You know, we hold up the letters and they point to them and spell out words. Anyway, we got it on paper. A last letter to you. It took *forever*." She touched my arm. "She had a lot to say—and she was *exhausted* at the end. Very short of breath. She just fell asleep."

"Did you hold her hand?"

"Yes." She nodded proudly. "I did. She wanted me to hold her 'real' hand because it had feeling, and then she asked me to hold the prosthetic hand because she said it might feel left out."

I looked at the paper, large trembly printing, and then the nurse's careful script.

Dear Digby,

I'm sorry I put you down as next of kin, but as you know, I have no one else. Willis, I'm not too happy about this, but I talked to God and she said: *You had a long ride on a broke-leg pony, Time to Get Off.* I am pretty tired anyway and it had to come, so please don't feel too bad and please stand up for me in court okay. You know more than anybody what I wanted to say, and, Willis, please *read* my journal. Also could you visit Nina; she won't understand what's happened. Maybe you could visit Danny too. He told me all about you as a kid and make no mistake, Willis, he is one high-style dancer. One last thing: I made up the story about my mother and the ice cream truck, and another: I know I am not beautiful. I am very, very, very ugly. But, Willis, my life was not bad. Read my journal. So forgive me, please. My motto: Don't backtrack in a snowstorm! Love forever,

Iris

P.S. Just for the record, I do *not* see a bright light that sees into my innermost soul. I see a carton of Häagen-Dazs on the Nurses' Station counter.
P.P.S. I would like to be buried in my gold running suit and my tie-dyed underpants, *no gravestone.*

Finally Terence and I were persuaded (as next of kin) to go down into the bowels of the hospital, to view The Body. But it wasn't Iris. It was just a grouping of body parts—like fruit arranged for a still life: an empty, stitched, expressionless face, closed eyes, wispy baby-fine colorless hair. One real flesh hand holding a prosthetic hand. It was only when I leaned closer to her that I saw one touching Iris-ism, the odd callouses on the palm flesh of the "good" fingers made by the plastic fingers clutching them for comfort, for relief from the terror and pain of the artificial extremity.

There was a private service on the Brookheart grounds. Iris's yoga instructor gave a kind of eulogy, and the all-patient orchestra played Don Ho favorites because that was all they knew. There was an altar set up with a photograph of Iris that obscured most of her face, and vases and vases of irises. She had already been buried in the Badger Falls cemetery. She hadn't wanted a graveside ceremony or gravestone. The patients were decked out in fairly festive attire—there were cowboy hats and plaid yarmulkes and a man in a World War I vintage pilot's togs, goggles, and an aviator's scarf, who sobbed and sobbed. Two of the women, who looked like aged twins, wore matching strapless tulle prom gowns with corsages. The dwarflike girl I'd seen at the Crafts Fair wore a miniskirt and saddle shoes and a lace mantilla.

Danny The Watcher was there, subdued in a white suit and shades. He waved to me. Nina, who looked the same as always, saw me and also waved; she came up to me after the service and looked right into my eyes. Her face was red and flushed from crying. *"Iris,"* she said and began to shake. "Where is Iris?" I looked for Terence, for help. He was signing autographs for the twin sisters. "Is Iris broken?" she asked.

The Cayman slithered toward us. "Hello." He smirked. "I'll take over now."

"No, *thanks*," I said and held Nina tighter. "We're fine." Nina frowned at him. *"Hey,"* she cried. "Bug off! This is *our* yard!" She sent a dark look after him. *"Seminal fluid,"* she confided in me.

We drove back to the city in silence. I had Iris's yucca plant on my lap, her Hot Line princess phone at my feet, and a couple pairs of her tie-dyes in my bag. After a while I fell asleep and dreamed something confused about Lily and Iris; I couldn't remember it when I woke up. I realized that I still hadn't managed to think of her as dead. When it was my turn to drive, I saw her once clearly at the side of the road, smiling and waving her plastic hand as we sped past at sixty-five mph, and then I saw nothing for miles and miles and miles.

Back at my apartment, Terence made some coffee in the kitchen, and I sat on the couch in the living room and shook out the sealed plastic bag of Iris's personal effects they'd given me. It contained Iris's polyurethane hospital I.D. bracelet with her blue-stenciled admission date, her name and social security number. The bracelet was tiny, infant-sized; it had been stapled around her prosthetic wrist. She had also brought with her a small stuffed animal—a monkey (made from a sock) with ripped arms and legs, a battered, stitched mouth, and one button eye hanging by a thread.

There were a few bottles of pills for various frightening physical ailments: anticoagulants, heartbeat regulators, Dilantin for seizures, nitroglycerine capsules. Finally, there was her wallet. It was rawhide leather, with hand-tooled cowboy curlicues and horses' heads. Inside there was her social security number, an I.D. card that listed me as an emergency contact, four intimidating medical information cards—and one photograph. It fell free from the dusty clear plastic it had rested behind for a long time—a three-by-five album snapshot from the early days of color film, late fifties maybe. It looked like a tiny neorealist painting: The grass was too green, the sky too blue. A pretty woman in her late twenties with bright red hair and dark eyes knelt on the grass in the front yard of a neat brick house, her arm around the little girl of five or so standing next to her. The woman smiled with such determined energy at the camera that she appeared in pain. The little girl was more restrained. She wore a Mickey Mouse T-shirt and white shorts and sandals. Her strawberry-blond hair fell to her waist in soft curls, her eyes were large and brown, her lovely five-year-old mouth was turned up in an unequivocal smile, but she ducked her head: She was shy. I recognized the clear intent of that face to fulfill its beauty, the humorous entreaty in those eyes. I kept the photo in front of me for a long time. Then I grasped that Terence was talking to me, taking the snapshot from my hand, holding it under the lamplight, grasped that I had been crying for a long time, that the child was gone now. Iris Moss was dead.

Nineteen

It was the second week of the Brookheart trial. The D.A. had indicted and formally charged five Brookheart staff members, including Basil Schrantz, on fifteen counts of sexual misconduct, assault, and rape. When I testified, I read Iris's letters aloud, and I recounted, in detail, her visit to me at SIS. The hypodermic needle was produced by Mr. Dorchek, the Assistant D.A. He asked me what it was, and I said it was the needle used to sedate Iris. The defense attorney, Mr. Brickmann, objected, and the objection was upheld. There was some discussion of prejudicing the jury, and I stood corrected—it was the hypodermic needle that Iris Moss had *told* me Basil Schrantz had used to sedate her. My testimony proceeded in a similar vein—me quoting Iris, the defense table qualifying Iris.

Mr. Brickmann cross-examined me. "Miss Digby, you *do* know that the recently deceased Iris Moss was a diagnosed victim of personality disorders who suffered occasional hallucinations? Dr. Rollo Bush, head of staff at Brookheart, described her in a routine case history file as 'incorrigible' and 'occasionally aggressive.' He says (and I quote): 'At times her seizures produced in her a euphoria and loquaciousness similar to that experienced by manic-depressives.' "

I said, "I did not know that Dr. Bush had used those particular adjectives to describe Iris, and I am not an expert on human psychology, but I *can* venture an opinion about why she might have seemed aggressive in his company. I spent ten minutes chatting with him, and his condescending manner made me want to wring his neck." The patients all laughed, and the Cayman, in the third row, glared savagely at me.

"Well, you and Ms. Moss must have made quite a pair. Ms. Moss recently shot someone while visiting you in your apartment, am I correct?"

"Yes, you are," I said, as Dorchek leaped up to object. "She was trying to save my life, as the New York Police Department and the newspapers have so clearly documented. If someone had broken into *your* apartment and held *you* hostage with a rifle, you'd find such behavior by a friend *heroic*, as I certainly did."

At a later point in the cross-examination, he held up a copy of the *Mirror* photograph of me in my tux and rabbit ears and asked me if I recognized it.

"Yes. That's me."

"In your *normal* working attire, as we're given to understand from this newspaper interview, which appeared in the *Mirror*"—he checked the date—"three and a half months ago. In the same interview you state, 'I'm crazy,' and you talk about how your column functions as a forum for 'crazy people.' "

"Yes, but I'd like to say—"

Dorchek objected, to no avail; the judge allowed the defense to proceed.

"And here is a photo of you (again in your rabbit ears) taken on the evening you and some other self-styled urban terrorists physically attacked Robert Hargill, the newscaster, at a Manhattan restaurant. As I understand it, you were carrying a .38 revolver. . . ."

"Your Honor," Dorchek said, "I must register my objection once again to this line of questioning—this is character defamation, and it serves no useful purpose in the trial proceedings."

"Sustained."

"Thank you, Miss Digby."

I watched the Cayman smile at me.

Then the patients testified: the boy who made the Playdough Jesus, the dwarfish girl, the prom-dress twins, a man who thought he was Lucky Lindbergh, Nina. They performed brilliantly. They told their brief, brutal stories in clear, un-self-pitying tones. They had been coached carefully by the prosecuting attorneys not to change the subject or become distracted, and for the most part they managed.

On the fourth day of testimony, Nina took the stand. She looked like the Little Match Girl in her patched red coat and boots. The prosecution led her quietly through her paces.

"You said you have been *hurt* sexually—how did this happen?"

"A man touched me; he came into my room at night."

"Were you afraid?"

She shuddered. "Yes. Afraid. I told him to go."

"What did the man do?"

"He *hurt* me, he gave me a shot, then he . . . touched me."

"Did this happen more than once?"

"This was many times, many, many. Since I was fifteen."

"And how old are you now, Miss Santos?"

"Nineteen."

"Is the man who came into your room all those times present here in the courtroom today?"

She pointed at one of the night-shift attendants, seated at a table with his lawyers. "That is the man.

"He covered my mouth with his hand and then he hurt me," she added, but the Assistant D.A. had already turned triumphantly toward the jury.

The cross-examination began. Mr. Brickmann approached the stand. "Miss Santos," he said, "when you say 'hurt' do you mean 'cause pain' or some other thing?"

"*Hurt*," she said emphatically. Her brown eyes, beneath her long bangs, searched his, trying to understand.

"Do you mean that someone touched you on the arm, *bumped* you, or pushed you roughly?"

She squinted hard at him, struggling to follow.

He pretended to bump into the courtroom railing. Then he held his knee. "Is this *hurt*?"

She looked at him blankly.

"Tell me then, please, what hurt is." He smiled at her patiently.

He was a large, fatherly, white-haired man, with piercing blue eyes and a hawk nose. An expensive navy-blue pinstripe suit. He had plenty of time.

She pointed through the red coat to her heart. "*Hurt.*"

The attorney smiled at her. "Your Honor," he said, "it seems clear to me that the witness is incapable of distinguishing one type of perceived 'hurt' from another. Unintentional rough treatment in the administration of an injection, for example, might seem to her to be a personal aggression, even a sexual aggression."

Dorchek was on his feet. "Objection, Your Honor! As stated prior to Miss Santos's testimony, she was born severely retarded, with Down's syndrome. She has limited powers of expression, approximately third-grade language capability—however, she can understand and communicate adequately if she is not frightened or *led*. I request that this harassment of the witness not be allowed to proceed."

Carol Muske-Dukes

186

"Overruled," said the judge. "But, Counsel, bear in mind that this witness must be addressed in a manner sensitive to her condition."

The white-haired attorney turned back to Nina—he gave her a dazzling capped smile.

"When the person who came into your room *hurt* you, Miss Santos, can you explain *what* he did to you? *Exactly?*"

Nina sat for a while looking around the court. She looked at me and smiled shyly. Her eyes crossed with effort. Then she lifted her hands, made a doughnut-hole with the thumb and second finger of her left and jabbed the second finger of the right in and out of it. She made a kissing sound with her lips. The other patients snickered.

"*Hurt,*" she said. "*Hurt.*"

Just then the twins rose in their places and pointed at the ceiling. "Look! Look!" they cried. Then they made a sort of clenched-jaw humming sound.

"What is it?" the Assistant D.A. called, eager to soothe them.

"Owl," they cried. "White owl!" The other patients looked nervous. Some looked up and stared, grim-faced. Others giggled and pointed to their temples. The defense team looked delighted. They looked up and nudged each other, whispering, "Owls! Owls!" The weird humming continued.

The judge gaveled for attention. The bailiff began moving for the twins. I looked up at the dark green vaulted ceiling with its rotting moldings. Then I looked at the twins. They ducked suddenly, as if a bird had dive-bombed them. Then they stopped humming and sat down.

The defense looked smug. Nina looked at me again and smiled. "Iris," she said in a loud, clear voice. "It's *Iris.*"

I did feel a change in the room, as if a fresh wind had blown through, clearing the air. Light poured suddenly into the diving chamber room from the high windows. A brief touch on my shoulder, like the brush of a wing, then it was gone. Did I imagine it?

"I don't think I did," I told Terence later. We were dining at a trendy night spot. My dinner looked like a Klee. "I think it really was Iris, her *spirit*. You know that wonderful heartbreaking moment in *A Death in the Family* when the father comes back for just a second, after the car accident, and the mother stands up and says, 'He's here,' and she follows him upstairs as he touches the sleeping heads of the children to say good-bye?"

"I think so. Do you want the rest of your free-ranging game hen?"

"No, take it. I mean, do you know what I mean?"

"That the dead communicate?" He spun my Klee gracefully onto his plate with his fork. He was trying to gain weight for a role. He was going to play a fat villain, Dirkley Crock, an evil country-western singer with a hairband, in an independent film.

"Do you think they do?"

He ate in silence for a bit. "I think Hamlet really *does* talk to and see his father, who is, of course, a ghost. I think the ghost is definitely there, not just Hamlet's imagination."

"Do you think Hamlet really goes crazy?"

"I think it's possible that Hamlet tries what that stewardess who wrote to you about putting toilet ice in passengers' drinks tried—a crazy safety valve."

When we got home, I looked through my mail. There was a letter and package from The Watcher, from Brookheart. Terence frowned and went off to bed—Danny Hayburn would never be his favorite person.

Dear Willis,
    You know that moment in *Franny and Zooey* when Zooey, as a kid, is up late one night and Jesus comes

into the kitchen and asks him for a *small* glass of ginger ale?

Well, tonight I went to sleep early (my neighbor in the next room had finally turned down the Whale Arias) and I had a dream about Iris.

She came into my room, sat down on the one straight-backed chair, and asked for a *small* Coke. I told her I didn't have one, and she grinned and said, "That's okay. Coke gives me gas!"

I started to tell her how glad I was to see her, but while I watched she simply faded away, smiling at me. I know it was probably nothing, but I feel so *much* better.

I'll be here another month or so. Would you ever come to see me? I'm nearly cured now! (My rear end *and* my psyche!)

Sincerely,
Danny
("The Watcher")

P.S. Here is a little something I thought you might be interested in. Do you remember that Iris kept a journal? Well, here it is! She told me about it and I know she mentioned it to you too. Well—it should have gone to you, as next of kin, as Iris designated, upon her death. But it disappeared. I saw Dr. Bush in her room the day before the funeral, putting together her personal effects to be distributed among her friends, according to her last wishes, which she wrote down. I asked you about the journal the day of the funeral service and you hadn't gotten it. So I did a little checking around—(*you* know I'm good at *that!*)

I see Bush every other day for a therapy session, and last Wednesday when I was in his office and he went out to pee and check his facial hair, I went through some of his drawers. (Not underpants, *file* drawers!) Sure enough, I found it. He had it in a manila pocket marked "Iris M." (I took out the journal, took a paperback from his shelf, put it in the folder to make it look like it was still there, and slid the journal under my shirt. *Just* in time!)

Why would the old Bushwacker want to keep a document that belonged to someone else? Well, I know. I've done some of my famous research around here— the patients haven't even begun to describe what they've suffered. Take a look at what's in the other package, if you can bear to.

Yours,

Dan

The journal was dark green leatherbound, with ruled pages inside like a child's notebook. I opened it at random.

March 11

I'm in the worst pain. It isn't just my head this time, but my heart and those bad nerves in my spine. They bring the pills when they feel like it. Is this really true, I wonder, or my imagination—I believe that Bush would do anything to cause trouble.

A bigger question—who is putting Tiger Balm on the Modess?

I saw the angel again tonight, sitting on the roof. The scene is set, she said to me. I asked for a little more time. She put sunglasses on, because all of a sudden she began to glow. My yucca plant turned three colors. "Iris," she said, "you're going to die and, boy, is it ever gonna hurt." "You better go back to heaven and learn a little diplomatic tact from Christ or a saint," I said. "Sorry," she said. "They usually put me on plane crashes. I'm not good at bedside."

And on another page, very close to the end:

Who is Danny? A real angel, messenger, or a demon? He looks like a rock star (but then, so do I!). We sit and talk and talk. Once he reached out and put his hand over my false hand, and then I put my other hand on his and he topped mine—just like kids, like a ceremony of kids. Like a kids' marriage.

Is he falling in love with me? God knows they all do. I haven't dressed up or even put on lipstick around him—it just doesn't seem right to paint your nails for someone you shot in the butt, does it?

Though all that's finished now—all that's been explained, and sometimes when I look at him I can see him as a child— the way I can with Digby. I think that's how you tell the good people in this world, you can still see the child.

Dalbert and the twins are really eager to start a radio show broadcast from here called "Dial a Fruitcake," but Danny thinks it would be misunderstood. And Bush, when he heard it, blamed Digby and me, of course! and all the "misleading publicity," the "unfocused spotlight" that we've shone on Brookheart and its residents. Well, when you shine a bright light an insect like Bush crawls out from under the rock.

Boy, is Bush mad about the way the hearings are going. They'll get rid of him if all this is proved. He hates me. When I walk down the hall past his office, I can feel his hate coming out, seeping under the door of his office and hissing like a green electric eel at my feet, curling around my ankles. Then it crawls up my spine. Pure hate. I always smile at him and he smiles back. Little hatchets come out of his eyes and chop at my eyes. Once he said to me, "I suppose you're pleased about the disruption you've caused." I said, "No. I will be pleased when we get new feminine hygiene dispensers in the ladies' rooms." "Iris," he said, "you're an unformed personality, you have no borders, it's fascinating and pitiable at once." "Bush," I said, "you are a border. You're a wall, a barbed-wire fence of a man." He laughed but not in a nice way. You know how Bush laughs: squealing black bats fly out of his mouth.

There were a lot of things crossed out, then:

I have to see Willis before I really start to go. Just to see her and hear her ridiculous laugh! She looks a lot happier now. I just hope that Terence doesn't fall in love with me. These things always do happen, but I'd just explain to him that she's my best friend and we can't have any of that. Anyway, Danny and I dance together in Classical Ballroom—like two swans. He had a problem with his seminal fluid, but it's amazing how he's recovered. Was it my bullet? I was interested in checking his genitals the night I shot him, to gauge the extent of the problem with his fluid, but Willis said no. I hope I get another chance to check.

Here comes Nina with the "new" coat they gave her. It's from Donated Goods, bottom of the barrel, after the staff people take what they want. It's not exactly Chanel, but I can work with it. I think I can use some of my tie-dyes for trim.

The pain is bad today. The pain is bad. I must call Willis. I want to show her other evidence. I have to talk to her soon, the angel is hanging around my door, and when I open it, she points at me and just smiles that shit-eating smile and says, "Are you ready? It's almost time, Iris. The scene is set."

Twenty

I couldn't make it to the trial every day, I had to go to work and answer letters (coming in thicker and faster than ever now that I'd gone so "public"), but I kept in touch with Mr. Dorchek, the Assistant D.A., by phone.

The case for our side was looking much less rosy than at the start of the trial. The patients had been impressive as witnesses, but a little confusing in places. (The patient who thought he was Lindbergh kept checking his watch on the stand, mumbling about "taking off" and "power head-winds.") Dorchek didn't actually say it, but I had been a real disappointment, I suspected. The questions about my dress and conduct had put me in the same uncertain category as the patient witnesses, even after re-cross-examination by the prosecutors.

Then it had turned out that the part-time physician who had been hailed as the ace prosecution witness gave a luke-warm testimony. It was damning to the defendants, but the guy waffled a little about what he had actually *seen*. However, the reporter who'd posed as a nurse had been superb, and Dorchek hoped *her* testimony would clinch it.

Then I got subpoenaed by the defense. On my way out to lunch, a scruffy little man handed me the papers. I called Dorchek right away.

"Jesus," I said, "I was such a terrible witness for *us*, *they* wanna use me for *their* side."

"Nah," he said, "but they're up to something. Don't worry. I'll sniff it out."

He called back later that afternoon. "Bush is their first witness, and I think they'll call you right after him. So what they want from you might be linked to what he says."

The next day in court I wore a prim gray wool dress and low-heeled shoes. My hair was tied in a mousy bun that would have made Miss Grundy proud. *And*, despite the lovely May weather, I put on a shapeless black coat. ("You look like a *nun*," said Terence.)

The Beatle-Cayman was called. He sat snuggled into the witness chair, picking at his muzzle.

Defense asked him questions about his career, about his tenure at Brookheart. Then they asked about the pornographic photographs taken of patients, discovered in an administrator's drawer.

The Beatle-Cayman said he wanted very much to see justice served, and *if*, in fact, what the patients said was true and accurate, he wanted to assist in bringing the perpetrators to light.

However, he said, it was his obligation to mention that patients occasionally did steal equipment and film from the photography classroom and take their own photographs. He said staff had confiscated "questionable" snapshots before— and put these items in files. The files were supposed to be clearly marked Confiscated Materials, but—he turned his warty hands upward in an appeal to the courtroom—"we're so busy," he said, "so understaffed and overworked, things get overlooked."

He and Brickmann built this premise quickly into a defense, then they got to Iris. The Cayman reiterated all he'd said before about the severity of her delusions. They they got to *me*.

"I saw *Miss* Digby, the day of our Crafts Fair at Brookheart. We spoke outside the institution as she was waiting for a taxi. She seemed nervous and disinclined to hear anything I had to say about Iris, who had just said good-bye to her. It seems to me that Miss Digby harbors an extreme hostility toward the male sex, which her recent exploits have certainly borne out."

"Objection."

"Sustained."

"What did you try to tell Miss Digby that day?"

"I *tried* to tell her that she had *gambled* in accepting Iris at her word in the matter of these alleged druggings and rapes by staff. Iris often imagined that things were happening to her that were not. I told Miss Digby this. I told her, for example, that Iris had invented a story about her mother that she often told people. Instead of admitting that her mother had killed herself and tried to kill her as well, an admission that would have been very painful—Iris said that her mother died in an accident."

"What was Miss Digby's response when you gave her this information?"

"She refused to believe me. She shouted at me."

It went on. I stopped listening for a bit.

I looked over at the jury. A nondescript gathering of men and women—but even numbers of each for once, I thought. One of the women looked back at me, hard, taking my measure. I adjusted my bun.

After Bush they put me on the stand.

"Miss Digby . . ." Brickmann began.

"Ms.," I whispered, but he didn't hear me.

"Dr. Bush has testified that he found your attitude toward Iris Moss irresponsible. You yourself apparently know that Iris Moss made things up occasionally. How do you justify having caused this . . . tempest when you could not verify the truth of anything Iris Moss said?"

"I don't need to justify anything. I merely submitted the facts, as they were given to me by Iris, to the *Mirror*. The *Mirror* sent a reporter who posed as a nurse to verify these facts, and apparently they were satisfied, after researching the situation that the patients were telling the truth."

"But Iris never gave you *facts*. She gave you her opinions as to what was happening. You believed her story about her mother, which has now been discredited. What guarantee did you have that she was capable of understanding the difference between an imaginary event and reality?"

"When Iris first wrote letters to me, I wasn't sure what *was* real to her, though I believed she had a good shit detector." I smiled apologetically at the jury. "She was very *aware*. But the day she came to see me at SIS, she came with evidence, a hypodermic needle in her hand, and she was clear about the wrongdoing. She knew the exact amount of sleep medication she'd been given, she'd even *saved* some. Chloral hydrate had never been prescribed for her—why was it being given to her? In *any* rape testimony, I assume the victim's statements must be considered as they are, without prejudice, *even* if the victim is a resident of a state hospital."

He asked me about the other stories Iris told.

"Iris was ugly and liked to say she was beautiful. Iris had a mother who tried to kill her, and she told people her mother was kind and lovely. Her face and her mother were horrible, and she could not change them, so she changed them in her mind—she made them *positive*—a crazy safety valve. The situation at Brookheart was a horrible situation, but not one that would *never* change—if it were, Iris, true to form, would have called it heaven. Putting chloral hydrate in her veins, a *negative* act, would not have been her way."

I looked at the man I was pretty sure was Basil Schrantz— a fattish man with a small head and pale eyelashes. He looked like a warhead. I thought I detected fear in his gaze. I hoped so.

Brickmann moved in for the kill. "Why don't you just admit, Miss Digby, that Iris Moss had no idea, really, what was going on, that you used her and used the ensuing scandal you caused for personal publicity?"

"Publicity?" I repeated.

"Publicity for yourself and your . . . magazine. You seem to thrive on it."

"Objection, Your Honor."

"Sustained."

He tried another tack. "Let's just assume, Miss Digby, for purposes of argument, that you *did* believe Iris Moss's story. Why is it that you called a newspaper, as opposed to a state investigative agency?"

"Which do you think would give *you* the fast response?"

There were a few titters.

"I would be grateful, Miss Digby, if we could stick to standard courtroom procedure and allow *me* to ask the questions here. When you made your decision to call a news periodical, you apparently stated unequivocally that there *was* sexual abuse of patients at Brookheart."

"I quoted Iris, who told me unequivocally there was, and *now* we have other testimony to corroborate—"

"We have 'testimony,' if you want to call it that—some confused and wandering patient anecdotes, a handful of blurry photographs that Dr. Bush has stated *may* have been taken by the patients themselves, and your *own* rather peculiar opinions about—"

"Objection!"

"Overruled."

"Your own rather peculiar opinions about human behavior. Would you describe yourself as a *man-hater*, Miss Digby? Do you think your feelings of animosity for male authority figures—I mean, look at your reactions to Dr. Bush—might have *colored* your own response to Iris's accounts of what happened to her?"

"I don't hate men. And I don't think men are completely inferior to women. I certainly don't believe that the missing leg of the Y chromosome has *anything* to do with the presence of, say, Sly Stallone in the world. Or Jesse Helms. That's just bad genetic luck, like getting Squeaky Fromme on the female side."

He looked genuinely perplexed. "I'm not sure I follow, Miss Digby. But your 'flights of fantasy' certainly help establish the extent to which you and the late Miss Moss *invented* this case together—"

"Objection! Counsel is prejudicing the jury!"

"Overruled. This is pertinent inquiry. But we will ask Counsel to limit remarks on personal behavior."

"Isn't it true," asked Brickmann, "that there is an element of fantasy to your testimony?"

"What about the *Mirror* reporter, Ms. McMahon?" I asked. "Her testimony included an eyewitness account of a rape."

"An eyewitness account of a male nurse whom Miss McMahon discovered appearing to straddle a female patient in bed . . . his testimony was clear: He was giving her a *back rub*."

He smirked at the jury. "Even Dr. Muller has modified *his* testimony."

"Dr. Muller," I said, "has modified his testimony because he was *threatened*." Before anyone else could speak, I pulled Iris's journal from my coat pocket and flipped it open. Brickmann objected right away, but I began to read loudly, blocking out his protests.

"I happen to be in possession of Iris Moss's daily journal," I shouted proudly. I waved the diary in the air, feeling like the Angel of Vindication. "Here is her entry for March twenty-ninth:

"*I slouched quietly outside Bush's office door like a spy, and like a spy I gathered intelligence. Bush spoke in a loud voice; I could hear every word. He was reminding Muller of a certain* shadow *on his record—*"

Brickmann was shouting at me, the judge was gaveling. I went on doggedly, raising my voice.

"*On two different occasions Muller apparently misjudged a dosage amount and put two patients in coma, who later died.*"

The judge instructed the bailiff to take the journal away from me. I read fast and loud.

"*The patient's names were Curran (or Cohen) and Morris. Bush's deal was this: I'll keep quiet about your malpractice if you lighten up on testimony—*"

The bailiff, a very stocky, perplexed-looking Japanese man, wrested the journal from my hands.

I faced the judge. "I don't understand. This is *evidence*, it tells us *why* Muller gave such a weak testimony."

The judge looked at the defense attorney.

Brickmann's face was bright red. "That is not *evidence*, that is *hearsay*, and hearsay is not admissible as testimony."

I could not believe my ears. "*Hearsay?* Are you kidding? This was Iris's private record of what went on at Brook-heart—she talks about medication schedules, her own illness, the feelings of the patients about the nursing care. . . . Why wouldn't the court listen to—"

Brickmann threw up his hands. "Your Honor, no further questions."

"Wait a minute," I called to him. "Are you saying that Iris *lied?*"

"Miss Digby." He turned toward me slowly, after smiling at the jury. "Iris Moss was a patient in a mental hospital. She could not distinguish the real from the imaginary. That is our whole argument. But, in any case, journals or letters, these are considered *hearsay.*"

"Iris was filled with *hope*, you see." I turned toward the jury, all of whom were looking at me with interest. "And that sometimes made her exaggerate. But you've heard Ms. McMahon's testimony, you've heard Muller—their statements concur with hers. And I have something *else* to show you. I didn't have time to show it to the prosecution yet, but—"

"Miss Digby, please step down. I have no further questions."

I pulled some papers from my coat pocket. "These, *these* will clinch the argument," I said. "Take a look, everybody, at these."

I held up the drawings Danny Hayburn had sent me. They looked like children's sketches; indeed, some were done in crayon; the colors were bright and the figures primitive. But the scene depicted in each was the same: nurses and doctors preying sexually on patients. One doctor in a white coat rose over a woman's bed like a vampire; his pointed teeth dripped blood; a huge balloonlike penis rose between his legs.

"I don't think you can see these clearly; I'll bring them over," I called to the jury.

The judge gaveled and shouted at Dorchek. "Counsel, please instruct your witness to leave the stand or she will be held in contempt."

"Willis." Dorchek moved toward me. "Please step down."

I lifted the drawings higher, leaning in the jury's direction.

"See? See the needles, the injections? See, this is a group rape here! Doesn't anybody see what these drawings mean? A current patient, Danny Hayburn, found them hidden in a file. They tell the whole story. They—"

"Bailiff!"

The bailiff hurried toward me. "Tell me," I shouted, "why these are not admissible."

The judge spoke slowly, in a terrible voice. "I am about to hand down a charge of contempt, do you understand? The prosecution has *rested* its case. This is the direct examination by the defense, and new evidence from the prosecution may not be introduced at this time, without petitioning the court." He glared at Dorchek. "The court is inclined to deny such a motion, should it be presented."

"Get down, Willis," Dorchek said.

I looked around me. I dropped my hands. I started to step down.

"But it's so *clear*, it's all so clear." One of the drawings fell free and fluttered to Brickmann's feet. He leaned down to pick it up and handed it to the bailiff, grim-faced, without looking at it. Some of the others fell, and I knelt down to pick them up. My bun came loose and my hair fell over my eyes. I began to cry. I looked again at the jury. "You should have known Iris—if only you could have heard her testify! They've made it sound like she couldn't *think*, couldn't comprehend what was happening to her. . . ."

"STEP DOWN, WILLIS."

I stepped down and sat in my chair in the third row, holding the drawings to my chest. People drew back from me. I sat and listened to the judge instructing the jury to "strike from memory" everything I had just said.

Twenty-One

A few days later I was sitting at my little red desk, piled high, as usual, with letters. Iris's yucca plant was barely visible behind one stack, but the picture from her wallet was pinned prominently to my bulletin board. Dresden Bostec was seated in my visitor's chair. Everyone else was at lunch, and she and I were contemplating one of her gooseberry pies, which she'd set on a checkered cloth between us. The pie was sunken—it looked like a human face a cow had stepped on.

"Maybe," Dresden trilled in her warbly old voice, "*that's* one of the reasons I never married. You know, so many of the other girls my age devoted their youth to acquiring domestic skills. I just never developed the concentration required to be a good cook.

"Who cares, though?" She shrugged, brightening. "I find that in my old age I can *bake pies* like Betty Crocker." She grinned at me and straightened her birdlike shoulders. She was wearing a flowered-print spring dress and a Mets baseball cap.

"Are you still going out with that guy?" I asked. "The one who loves your pies?" I handed her a Styrofoam cup of coffee.

"He's not too well. Had a little problem with his colostomy bag last week. He had dinner at my place on Tuesday and—"

"Did you serve one of your pies?"

"Of course. He ate three pieces, we went dancing, and, lo and behold, the next day his bag went on the blink, if you'll excuse my French." She paused for effect. "He's a lot younger than me too—seventy-two. They just can't keep up."

She took a plastic knife and a paper plate out of her purse. She cut out a wedge of pie, put it on the paper plate, and slid it toward me. I looked at it.

"You'll have to forgive me, Dresden. I'm not very hungry. I keep thinking about the trial."

The jury had been out three days, and we were expecting a verdict today. I was not expecting a vote of confidence. Every time I'd tried to say what I thought Iris would have wanted said, I'd defied due process. Yet the defense was able to mop up the stand with *me*. Dorchek was still hopeful; I'd just spoken on the phone to him, but he sounded strained.

"You need cheering up, I can see," said Dresden. "That's why I brought you something for your Letters Hall of Fame."

I had personally annexed a section of bulletin board in the hall near my office and posted some of my All-Time Letters. There were a couple of Dino Pedrelli's, two from the stewardess, two from the U.F.O. expert, one from the King of New Jersey, from the woman who fed cat food to her husband, from Bea Plotkin, a recent one from The Watcher (which simply said, "I'm cured! Will you marry me?"), a recent one from W.I.T.C.H., making me an honorary lifetime member, a very recent one from Terence ("I'm *not* cured! Will you *stay* married to me?"), one from the Pissed-Off Chef:

"Now here's an hors d'oeuvre *guaranteed* to get rid of late-staying cocktail guests. I call them Death Weenies," and one from Bob Hargill, suggesting that I stop my "reign of terror." (Every time I sang along with the radio now, Page demanded I stop my "reign of terror.")

Dresden ferreted in her big needlepoint carpetbag and brought out an ancient-looking letter. It was dog-eared, yellowed with age, bearing a stained and peeling stamp. (I strained to see it, *one cent*?)

"You know, Willis," she said, "I was thinking about you and your tie-up with W.I.T.C.H. the other day. I don't know *why* they don't ask *me* to join! I could have helped the night you got after Hargill. I look better than that sad sack, and I'm"— she paused—"can't quite remember now. Eighty-three?"

We drank our coffee in silence for a bit. "Yes," she said emphatically. "Eighty-*three*. I was just remembering 1917—the year this letter was sent to me. It's from my older sister Lillian," she said, and showed me the spidery handwriting on the envelope. "She was very strong in the Movement, you know, Lillian. She was twenty-two, and I was only fourteen, awkward and gangly. I had two other sisters, but she was the passionate, smart one *and* the beauty, too! That was a *violent* time, when they chained themselves to the White House gates and to the wheels of important men's carriages. The marches here in New York got rough. Dear Lord, I remember coming home from school once and finding her standing at the window in the parlor, her long brown hair shining down her back. Then she turned around. Someone had flung mud all over her, from head to toe, her white dress and her 'Votes for Women' shoulder banner were *covered* with dark smears. She had been crying, I could tell. She came up to me, and I remember being a little afraid of her. 'Dressy,' she cried, and took me by the shoulders. 'Look at me. They threw handfuls of sludge at us—men, women,

even *children*. They're so *afraid*.' Take a forkful of *pie*, Willis,"
she suggested. I shook my head.

"Later she went down to Washington and was there when
they arrested Alice Paul on the White House steps, took her
to jail and sentenced her to seven months—which is when
she began her hunger strike. That's what this letter *starts*
with, the arrest of Alice Paul. She wrote it to me from *Washington*." She pointed to the pie again, and again I demurred.
She opened the old letter and began to read aloud:

"Dear Dressy,

"Well, here we are, back at Mrs. Kramer's after the
most extraordinary day of my life! We are having hot
cups of soup and coffee, drying our clothes—and I
thought I would write to you, dear little sister.

"You've expressed interest in history and in this great
Cause—I charge you now to remember this day—the
day they took Alice Paul to prison from the White House
steps! Our shamed president said nothing. The crowd
screamed, 'Traitors!' and 'Turncoats!' the way they have
all through the War, and they threw stones at us.

"Well, dear, we tried to sing our songs and keep our
spirits up, but then a large fat man in the crowd threw
a stone and hit Theresa in the neck. She fell, but recovered herself. 'Where are your husbands?' the fat man
shouted. 'Where is your wife—she needs *us*!' we called
back. 'Madam! No wife of mine would march in a monkey line!' he cried out. Oh, Dressy, you should have
heard them then—the other men started jeering, 'Monkey line! Monkey line!' and 'Get back to your kitchens
and your mending! Get back to your neglected children—or are you all barren? Spinsters!' they cried.
'Hags!'—the worst epithets men think to call the fair
sex. One man left a rearing horse he'd been beating in

the street and snapped his bloody whip smartly in the air, yelling, 'This tongue would talk sense into them!' And the others cheered—I recall particularly the faces of the policemen, for whom this provided great merriment. They pushed the crowd back halfheartedly and laughed heartily at our expense.

"Then the horsewhip man called out, 'And *what* would you creatures make of the right to cast ballot?' And Miss Turner, who reads law and history, cried, 'Our cause grew from the abolitionist—would you have woman *stay* slaves and go without representation in a democratic land?' And the cursed man—Dressy, I hope not to injure you with this, but he looked right and left, then shouted, 'Niggers and slatterns, slatterns and niggers—you say? Well, that is a monkey line—if *I* do say!' He turned to his comrades, who all held their sides with laughter.

"And then Constance Dalton, of our company, who is a mulatto, came forward and stood front of the line, to face this man. 'Sir?' the brave woman called out. 'Are you suggesting that I should be ashamed of my skin— and my sex? Come forward,' she said, 'and say what it is you mean to my *face.*'

"There was a low rumbling that started deep in the crowd, and when I heard it, Dressy, I was very frightened. I saw the man move toward her with his whip, and I felt her flinch. And suddenly I felt *lifted up*, free in such a manner I cannot explain. I made a face, I made a *monkey face* at the unfortunate men, since they'd called us a *monkey line*—then all the women began making faces, sticking out their tongues, cawing and shrieking, putting their thumbs in their ears and waggling their fingers. A fine display!

"The men fell back. They were frightened, as if they'd suspected this to be the way women had always *wished* to behave—like wild creatures. Their expressions were horrified, as if they expected us to tear off our corsets and swing from the trees! Oh, Dressy, we might *have!*"

"Willis, have a piece of that pie!" she commanded, interrupting herself. "It's got a flavor you won't believe! Willis, you want to know why men fear women? My sister says it later in this letter," she said, folding the pages into the envelope. "Because we're *anarchists,* deep inside, anarchists to a woman! Anarchists for *love. EAT THAT PIE!*" she bellowed.

I jumped to, digging in with the plastic fork. She watched me carefully. "Elizabeth Cady Stanton took a scissors and cut a law from the books of her father, the judge, because it said men could sell property out from under women and she'd heard a poor woman weeping over it in his chambers. She was only ten when she did it. Anarchists!" She stuffed a big piece of pie in her mouth and spit a little out as she talked. "Those women could have taught W.I.T.C.H. some tricks!"

I put on my rabbit ears; I just felt a need to suddenly.

"You know, Willis," she said, leaning forward a little, whistling through her teeth and spitting pie crumbs, "I've never liked that damn contraption you wear on your head. It makes you look *goonish.*"

"Dresden," I said, and took the letter out of her old thin hand and kissed it, then pinned it up next to Iris's wallet snapshot, "I can't *stand* your pies." I took the fork and stabbed the loathsome confection. "They're *vile.*"

The phone rang. I picked it up and said, "I'm an Anarchist for Love, and I'm on my way to lunch. Talk fast!"

Mr. Dorchek, the Assistant D.A., said, "Is this fast enough? Our good jury of peers came back with a winning vote for us. They took 'em down on eleven counts! Not bad."

I hugged Dresden, then I picked up Iris's Hot Line to the Supreme, Somewhat Preoccupied Intelligence, and said, "I *believe*," and hung up.

Dresden was waiting patiently to finish our conversation. She looked down at her bilious creation. "You're right," she said. "My pies *suck*. But look at all the friends I've made, Willis, because of them! *Think* about it."

Then we went out together for a couple of beers, Dresden and I—we left the pie on Holly's desk, and I, not being one to backtrack in a snowstorm, left the rabbit ears behind me.